5 Thr

Characte

- Woodsey 15 years old

Hobbies: playing football, boxing for local club; Thingwall boxing club and history. Can be funny at times. Dark hair, blue eyes, 5ft 7" tall, athletic build

- Gaffo 15 years old

Hobbies: 3rd dan martial arts, playing football and a good dancer, very dry wit, strawberry blond hair, blue eyes, 5ft 7" all, athletic build

- Mayo 15 years old

Hobbies: playing football and boxing for Thingwall boxing club. Dark hair, blue eyes, loyal to his friends. 5ft 5" tall, athletic build

- Chrissy 15 years old

Hobbies: playing football, playing tricks on everyone, very funny. Brown hair blue eyes, 5ft 6" tall, slim and nimble.

- Campbell 15 years old

Hobbies: playing football, body building, likes blowing things up with gun powder from fire-works, the quiet one, street fighter. Brown hair, blue eyes 5ft 7" tall, stocky build, but fast

5 THROUGH TIME

Written by Terence George Woods

Introduction

The sound of an alarm rings at the side of Woodsey's bed, his eyes slowly open and his hand taps the top of his clock.

"Arrr" and yawns with his arms stretched out, he then hears his dad's voice.

"Come on lad, time to get ready, we've got to be out by 5 30 am."

"Okay dad I'm up." it was 5 am so Woodsey had half an hour to get ready.

His dad had his own haulage business collecting and delivering fruit and veg and in the summer months. Woodsey loved helping his dad, for a few quid, obviously.

"Come on lad let's get going."
His mum called from the top of the stairs, "Les don't forget your butties in the fridge."

"Okay Frances, we've got them, see you later."

As they arrived at the fruit and veg market on Edge Lane Liverpool, Woodsey's eyes lit up at the hustle and bustle of the market. They would park the car and make their way over to the wagon to warm the engine up. Dad would go the stalls and get the orders for the day and we would head off to the warehouses to pick up many different pallets of fruit and veg for the farmers and the fruit stalls.

The days always went over quickly for Woodsey, as he loved meeting different people from all the warehouses and market stalls. It was soon 12 o'clock and the working day was nearly over. Dad gave him the job of unloading the wagon with the forklift truck. This was Woodsey's favourite part of the day, as well as getting to drive his dad's old Mercedes car around the market.

"You are getting good at driving son, soon you will be taking me home."

"I can't wait, said Woodsey.

"Where are you going today then son?"

"I'm meeting all my mates for a game of footy in Dovecot park."

" Okay, enjoy yourself, but try and get some sleep today, don't wear yourself out".

"Who are you meeting today."

"Err, Gaffo, Chrissy, Mayo and Campbell".

"They are nice lads them lot."

As we pulled up outside our house in Newenham Crescent, Knotty Ash, Chrissy was already there. Dad said,

"Alright Chrissy."

"Hello Mr Woods," said Chrissy.

Mum opened the door. "You've got ten messages

from your mates, seven from Chrissy, oh! hello Chrissy- you are already here- and three more I've written them down on the notebook."
Woodsey went to the phone table to read the messages on the notebook. They all said the same thing, meet at Dovecot park at 1. 30 pm.

CHAPTER ONE

It was the summer of 1981 when life would change forever for five young men from Knotty Ash, Liverpool.

And so, the story begins. It was 5 August 1981 during the school holiday. It was warm that day and all the lads were making their way to Dovecot park to have a kick about with a battered old case ball. They all enjoyed the park, especially as there were only three weeks left of the summer holidays until their final year at St Margaret Mary's School, Pilch Lane, Liverpool.

They were all at the park for about an hour playing footy (football), when they decided to stop for a drink. They were all lying down under the warm sunlight, the park was very busy and there was a group of girls nearby with a radio on and it was playing the latest hit by the Jam, it was called,(Funeral Pyre).

"Nothing better than this," said Woodsey, "lying down with the sun on your face and listening to The Jam."

Then he suddenly joined in the chorus. "In the funeral pyre and watch the flames growing higher, but if you get too burnt, you can't come back home".

Then all the lads joined in. As they were all singing, Woodsey noticed something. "What's that over there?" Chrissy answered back. "What? What are you looking at?"

"That over there," Woodsey said again, "it's like a cloud on the floor, with little lights coming from it."

"Oh yes," said Mayo.

Then all of them could see it. As they all stood together looking at this strange image, they were all drawn closer to it. They soon realised they were only a couple of feet away from this see-through shimmering mist.

"Hold on lads," Gaffo said, "have you noticed that the park is totally empty except for us lot?"

"It's the first time I've seen Dovecot park empty while the schools are off," said Campbell.

All the lads just looked at each other wondering just what was going on. With a bit of fear and excitement in their eyes, Chrissy made the first move and put his hand towards the mist. Suddenly, his hand was sucked in up to his wrist. Chrissy started shouting, "I can't get my hand out!" and the more he struggled the worse it got.

It was soon up to his elbow and you could see the panic on Chrissy's face. That's when Woodsey grabbed hold of Chrissy's waist and tried to pull him out, but it wasn't working. Before they knew it, Woodsey was holding on to Chrissy, Gaffo was holding on to Woodsey, Mayo was holding on to Gaffo and Campbell was holding on to Mayo. So, there they all were in a row trying to cling on to each other and within a flash they were all sucked in, spinning around in darkness,for what felt like ages.

It was a strange feeling, although it was dark, they could all still see each other, all in a circle spinning around. Then all of a sudden it was like they were lowered to the ground onto a hard pavement, all still in a circle. Campbell was the first

to speak as they all gasped for breath. "What was that? What's just happened?"

They all just looked at each other, wide eyed and shaking their heads.

Chrissy said, "I don't know about you lot, but that's the best ride I've ever been on."

Mayo said, "Trust you to touch that thing first," They all laughed.

The lads were trying to come to terms with what had just happened when they realised that they were not in Dovecot park anymore, but in a built-up area that none of them recognised. As they looked round, they could see people walking towards

them, but they were wearing old fashioned clothes and top hats and some younger kids looked like street urchins.

As a man walked past them, Woodsy said,

"Hey mate, are you making a film."

The man replied in a London accent,

"What are you saying."

"You know, like a period drama. Like Jane Austen."

The man replied, "I don't know what you mean."

Mayo stepped in saying?"

"Okay mate, if you're not making a movie, where the hell, are we?" The man looked at them with a puzzled look.

"You are in London," he answered.

"London," Gasped Gaffo. "What the hell are we doing in London."

The man looked more puzzled, he asked,"Where are you from then?"

"Liverpool," replied Campbell.

"Didn't think you were from around here, anyway must be on my way."

"Before you go," said Woodsey, "what year is it?"

"Its 1752," replied the man," good day to you." and off he went.

"1752? What's going on?" said Gaffo, "I don't understand this."

Woodsey was deep in thought. "We must have slipped through time somehow."

"Why have we ended up in the smoke," asked Chrissy.

"I don't know," said Woodsey, "but if it is 1752 then King George II is in charge on the throne.

"Who is the Prime Minister then?" asked Mayo.

"It's Pelham for another two years," said Woodsey.

"I didn't think your knowledge of history would ever come in so useful," said Gaffo.

"You just stick to your kung fu, I think we are going to need it," said Woodsey, with a slight smile on his face.

The lads tried to gather their thoughts of what had happened to them and how they were going to get back home and to the right year. It was all looking very gloomy and bleak for the lads. A strange feeling was hanging over the five young men from Liverpool, as to what to do next and now knowing they had slipped through time, they were the ones that looked odd and out of place. As they looked around all they could see were London folk from over two hundred years ago, in their top hats and smart clothes and the not so privileged in rags.

Campbell said, "We must look out of place, they are all gawping at us."

Chrissy replied, "Well I don't think they have seen adidas, samba trainers, Lacoste jumpers or bleached washed denim jeans before".

"I gathered that much funny arse."

Mayo let out a big sigh. "Where are we going to stay tonight. if we don't manage to find our way back? Plus we haven't got any money."

"I've got some money," said Gaffo.

"I think Mayo meant today's legal tender," said Woodsey,

"we will need to move on and try and find somewhere we can get our heads down for the night and get some grub."

"I wonder if there are any hostels?" Chrissy said.

"Not in this place You are more likely to be sent to a workhouse." Woodsey replied.

"Sod that," said Gaffo, "no one is sending me to a workhouse."

All the lads let out a nervous chuckle.

Woodsey shouted out to a young lad wearing scruffy old clothes.

"Come over here a minute."

He answered back in a London accent.

"Who, me?"

"Yes, you."

You could see he was a bit apprehensive to approach as the lads looked strange to him.

"What's your name?" asked Woodsey.

"Fig," he replied.

"Okay Fig, nice to meet you."

"Where are you all from?"

To which Chrissy replied, "1981."

"Ignore him, we are all from Liverpool."

Fig replied, "Oh yes I've heard of Liverpool, it takes days to get there, what are you doing in London?"

"It's kind of a mad story, we will tell you another time." Gaffo said.

"Anyway," said Woodsey, "this is Gaffo, Chrissy, Mayo and Campbell, and I'm Woodsey.

"Nice to meet you all."

Campbell asked Fig was there anywhere they could get some sleep and some scran.

Fig asked, "what's scran?"
Chrissy told him it was food in scouse. Fig told them there was, but they would have to help out in the inn where his mum worked.

"Sounds like a good deal to me," said Mayo. Fig asked the lads how old they were, Woodsey told him they were all fifteen.

"Fifteen," Fig said, "you are all tall with the bodies of men." *They asked Fig his age and were shocked to hear he was sixteen, because Fig was so small and skinny.*

"You need a good pan of scouse down your neck." said Chrissy.

"What's scouse?" asked Fig.

"It's stew or broth," said Campbell.

"Follow me," said Fig.

So off they all went, walking on the old cobblestones, with horses and carts rattling along the bumpy roads. It was a very dense place, with a misty fog hanging in the air. There was a strong smell of smoke from the industrial and house chimneys.

CHAPTER TWO

Fig asked the lads again *what their story was and what kind of clothes they were wearing.* Woodsey looked at Fig and
said," Listen, I know this is going to sound strange, but we have been dragged here from another time."

"What do you mean, another time?" asked Fig.
Woodsey looked at all the lads, they nodded, as if to say, you need to tell him, so Woodsey explained to Fig that they were from 1981, over two hundred years in the future. Fig looked puzzled. Gaffo then pulled a five-pound note from his pocket and said, "Here Fig have a look at this. It's a five-pound note from 1981, It's got the date on it and the head of Queen Elizabeth II."
Fig was amazed by this and you could instantly see the belief in his eyes.

"You will have to keep quiet about this Fig," said Woodsey, "we don't want to bring unwanted attention to us."

"I understand," Fig said.
Gaffo looked at Fig. "You can give me my fiver back now. I will need that when we get back home."

You could see Fig was amazed by what he had just seen and asked how we came to have so much money!

“Five pounds? We can earn that in a day,” said Mayo.

Fig replied, “It would take me years to earn that sort of money, I am lucky if I earn a halfpenny a day.”

“Half a penny,” Mayo gasped, “What could you buy with that?”

Woodsey said, “You will be surprised what you can get with a halfpenny.”

As they carried on walking Woodsy said to Fig, “If your mum does let us stay, she will want to know why we are dressed so differently.”

“It’s okay, I will just tell her this is the way people dress from Liverpool.

Chrissy laughed. “She will think all people from Liverpool wear tight jeans and trainers haha!”

Fig told the lads they were not far from the inn. Campbell suddenly said, “I feel as if someone has been watching us since we got here.”

“What makes you think that?” said Fig.

“I don’t know, it just feels like we have got eyes on us. I feel like everyone has eyes on us.”

“That’s because they do,” said Fig, “nobody has ever seen your footwear, clothes or your funny hair before.”

“What do you mean?” said Woodsey, “this is my best wedge cut haha!"

When they arrived at the inn Fig told the

lads that it was called the Ship Inn, not far from the Thames.

Chrissy said, “My God, I hope we don’t get press ganged.” Fig thought this was funny, as this was a possibility. Campbell said, “Yeah I bet we all wake up on a ship tomorrow, tied up." Fig started to laugh and told them not to worry, they would be safe with him.

Fig led the way through the front door of the Ship Inn, the lads followed behind him. Fig shouted

to his Mum, “Mum is it okay for my friends to spend the night in my room?”

“Of- course dear, but they will have to earn their keep.”

“Okay Mum, this is Woodsey, “Hi”

Chrissy// “Hi”

Gaffo// “Hi”//

Campbell// “Hi”// and Mayo//"Hi. “This is my mum, Rose.”

Rose was a hardworking woman in her early forties, but beneath the old clothes and hard life, she was an attractive woman with flame red hair and green eyes. Woodsey looked around the inn, it was full of hard done by working class people with a few ragamuffins thrown in.

“Well lads we are the centre of attention again.” Everyone was looking at the lads.

Rose asked, “where are you from?”

Fig replied, “Liverpool Mum.”

“Oh, I know a man from Liverpool.”

"Okay Mum, I will show my friends where they can sleep tonight." Fig showed the lads his room, it was small with one bed so they would have to make themselves comfortable on the floor. *The lads accepted, after all it was only for one night!*

Gaffo asked Fig who else lived at the inn. Fig told them himself his mum and sister but with a sad look on his face he paused for a bit, then he told them his dad had died, just nine months before when he was trampled by a horse.

"I'm sorry to hear that Fig," said Gaffo.

"it's okay I just look after mum now."

Chrissy asked Fig how old his sister was.

"She is 18," Fig replied, "and you can keep your eyes off her."

Just as Fig finished his sentence, the door opened, and his sister Mel looked around the door.

Mayo looked at her and said, "You are beautiful."

Campbell said, "Do you know you have just said that out loud, Romeo?"

Mel was beautiful, a younger version of her mum with the same flame red hair and green eyes.

Mel said, "Just come to check on your friends and Mum said she needs you downstairs."

Fig said, "Come on, we best go and do our chores."

So, they all went down- stairs and were surprised to see a table with six bowls of broth and bread sticks with a jug of ale.

Rose shouted, "Go on lads, eat up. I have plenty of work for you to do later."

All the lads sat down and tucked into their broth.

Campbell said, "Hey it's not bad this."
Chrissy said, "I don't know about the bread though, it is rock hard, you could knock a nail in with it." He started to bang the bread stick on the table. It made a very loud noise and they all burst out laughing, even some of the locals laughed. Woodsey said, "Just soak it in your broth, it will be okay." Mayo took the first swig of the ale and spat it out. "Bleeding hell. That's worse than the mild at the Boundary pub!" Campbell started laughing, "just get it down you, you, big girl's blouse."
Fig was finding all these strange sayings quite amusing. "Right then," said Fig, "we need someone to sweep the floors".
"I'll do that," said Gaffo.
"I need two to help me collect the plates and jugs."
"I'll do that," Campbell said
"and so, will I," said Chrissy."
"Woodsey and Mayo can work behind the bar with mum and Mel."
"No problem," said Mayo. Woodsey looked at Mayo and said, "Come on then Romeo, let's get to work."

As the inn got busy the lads were mixing with the locals as they worked, but they were still getting some strange looks, which they expected, later on, a man walked in and everyone fell silent, even Rose looked worried. Woodsey said, "Who is this bloke?"
Rose said, "Just don't upset him, he is a bad man,

his name is Jacks and he is a troublemaker."
Woodsey looked at Jacks. He was tall and skinny, but not much taller than the lads. He had black teeth with long black greasy hair and his breath could knock you sideways. Woodsey gave a glance to all the lads and they all nodded back, as if to say *they had noticed him*. They were all aware that there was fear around the inn. Rose explained to Woodsey and Mayo behind the bar that it wasn't just Jacks, he had a few cronies around the Inn, and they would intimidate people, so keep on Jacks side.
Woodsey said to Mayo, "Take a walk around the pub and let the lads know this Jacks bloke is not on his own."
Mayo made his way around the inn, to let everyone know. Fig came over to the bar with the look of
terror in his eyes and spoke to his sister, "Mel go upstairs. We have enough people to work tonight."
"No," said Mel, Mum needs me. But you could see Mel was upset by the presence of this man.

Jacks made his way to the bar and slammed a halfpenny on the bar, "Give me some broth and ale wench and be quick about it."
Rose gave Jacks his food and ale. The next thing Gaffo slammed the brush into Jacks foot, "Oh sorry mate, just sweeping this shit off the floor."
Jacks replied, "Just watch where you are going."
Woodsey knew what Gaffo meant by' *sweeping the*

shit off the floor' and had a giggle to himself.

Things settled for a little while, but then Jacks was soon back at the bar.

"I need more ale," said Jacks, slamming his hand on the bar.

Mayo walked over and asked, "what are you having?"

"I don't want you to serve me boy, I want Rose. or Mel would be even better."

Mayo looked at Jacks with a steely stare. Rose rushed over quickly to stop any aggro.

"Okay Jacks, what are you having?"

"You, for a start." He put his hand on her cheek and his hand moved down and brushed her breast. Rose pulled away from Jacks with disgust.

Gaffo shouted out loud. "Hey knobhead, leave Rose alone." Jacks looked at Gaffo and said, "what's a knobhead?"

Well, you have a knob between your legs, but yours is on your head."

Jacks eyes screwed up with anger. "You dare mock me boy?" Gaffo replied, "whatever." A few cronies started to come out from the shadows.

Woodsey and Mayo jumped over the bar. Rose said, "It's okay Jacks, I don't want any trouble to-night."

Jacks replied, "I think it's too late for that."

Chrissy and Campbell made their way over as they could see trouble brewing. Although only 15, they were all well-built and athletic.

Jacks stood back to let his men do the fight-

ing for him. there were seven of them including Jacks, who was in a fixed stare with Gaffo. Woodsey and Mayo took their boxing stance.
Chrissy looked over and said, "It looks like you are doing the Queensbury rules."
Just as he said that one of the men threw a punch at Chrissy, which just glanced off his face. Chrissy jumped on the man's back and forced him to the floor. Campbell was swinging his arms like a mad man and caught one man right in the face, knocking him clean out. Woodsey and Mayo were taking on two men with precision, both ducking out of the way and jabbing them into submission. In the end only Jacks was standing.
Gaffo said, "Your turn." Jacks ran at Gaffo. He just brushed Jacks side and did a full round house kick to his temple and wiped him out. A few of Jacks mates were coming around and carried Jacks out. Suddenly there was a big cheer from all the locals and the boys were the toast of the night. Fig, Rose and Mel were amazed at how quickly the boys had put all the men down and without breaking any tables or chairs. Rose said, "What can I say. You are all welcome to stay as long as you need to. No one has ever done that to Jacks and his men."
Chrissy said, "How easy was that' They can't fight for toffee." "Well you are the only one with a black eye out of all of us," said Campbell.
"It was a lucky punch," said Chrissy.

The lads were starting to get a lot of attention. Mayo was happy just chatting to Mel, but

all the others were drinking ale bought by the locals Chrissy, Gaffo, Woodsey and Campbell were all getting attention from the ladies of the night, who were happy with what happened to Jacks.
One of the girls sat on Chrissy's knee and said, "How about we go and have a good time?"
Chrissy leaned over to Gaffo and whispered in his ear. "When do they invent toothpaste? My God, her breath stinks poor girl."
Gaffo said, "You will have to ask Woodsey, he is the history man."

Rose shouted, "Right come on boys, it's time to get some rest. The lads made their way to the bedroom. Just before they got behind the bar, a tall Chinese man grabbed Gaffo by the arm. "Where did you learn those moves?"

"Toxteth," Gaffo replied. "And what country is that?"//

"It's not a country, it's in Liverpool,"// "but which art is if from."

"Well, it's Kung Fu Karate and Jujitsu."

"That's amazing," the man said, "I hope to speak to you again soon."
"Who is that?" asked Woodsey, Gaffo replied

"Just some bloke from China asking about martial arts. Come on, let's get some sleep. I don't think sleeping on the floor is going to be a problem."
when they got to the room, Mel had put blankets on the floor, which made it much more comfortable.

All the lads were fast asleep from their long day,In the morning Chrissy was the first to wake up and let out a big yawn. He was so loud he woke everyone up.
Campbell sat up. "My back is killing me.He let out a big fart,and all started laughing. Fig couldn't stop laughing, he thought it was the funniest thing ever.
Woodsey said, "My God that stinks, smelly arse!" This just made Fig laugh even more.
Chrissy said, "I need a wee, where is the toilet?" Woodsey started laughing, "Sorry Chrissy, there are no toilets around yet, you will have to piss in that pot over there."
"What, in that pot?"
"Yes," said Fig.
"And where do I put the piss?"
"Throw it out of the window," Fig said.
"This is getting worse, what if I need a crap?"
"Well, you take it outside and put it in the gutter," said Fig.
"Everyone is getting a history lesson today," said Woodsey.

All the lads got ready to start the day and help Rose with the inn. When they came downstairs, they could see a table set out for them with bread and what looked like butter and water. Although it wasn't
what the lads were used to, they did appreciate what Rose had done for them.
"Here you go my heroes, a nice jug of water for

you all.

Listen boys," Rose said, "you are going to have to be careful you don't get any comeback from Jacks and his men.

"Don't worry about them, if they try it again, we will put them down the same way," said Campbell.

Mayo said, "I think your locals will back us up, if any more trouble starts."

"Yes, I think you're right. With you lot in here, I don't' think anyone would go against you,"

"Right," said Rose, "Fig show your friends around the Thames, there is no work to do around here for a few hours."

"Can Mel come?" said Mayo.

"Not today," said Rose, "I need her to help me clean the inn rooms for the customers."

You could see Mel was disappointed, but she knew her mum needed her. You could see she had feelings for Mayo. Gaffo said, "Come on then, let's go and see the sights."

Fig led the boys out of the ship inn and on to the busy streets again. No sooner had they got out of the door, they were the center of attention again some gave strange looks, and some gave friendly looks especially from the people who were at the ship Inn the night before.

"All right boys," some of people were saying and waving to them.

All of a sudden, a man appeared with a black eye patch and a seafaring hat, like a character from a pirate movie. He grabbed Mayo's hand and said, "That's a pretty gold ring," it had a sovereign coin on it," I think I will have this ring, it is worth a lot of money."

Gaffo said, "What about my ring,

"What ring?" the man asked.

"This one," Gaffo poked him straight in his good eye.

The man let go of Mayo's hand and started screaming. The lads just walked away laughing.

Campbell was starting to feel a bit concerned. Mayo could see that he was worried about something.

"Are you okay Campbell?"

"No, I've got that feeling that we are being watched."

"Don't worry Campbell," said Chrissy, "we will be just fine." The thing was, Woodsey was feeling the same as Campbell. There was definitely a presence around the lads, but what it was, he couldn't work out.

As they all walked along the docks, the lads were amazed by the sights of the docks and the old ships. They were all seeing history for real right in front of their eyes. Woodsey said, "Take it all in lads, this is great."

Fig was happy that his new friends were happy and excited at what they were seeing.

Fig had an idea. "Listen everyone, I do some work for Mr Dobbs and he is a wealthy man and a bit mad. Maybe he would be interested in your story."

"I don't know," said Woodsey, "when you say mad, what do you mean?"

"He is an inventor and a writer," said Fig.

"Sounds like a plan to me. Can't see us getting home anytime soon, so let's go and see this nutter," said Gaffo. They all agreed and made their way there.

Fig said, "Let me talk to Mr Dobbs first before he meets you lot, don't want to make him nervous."

As they made their way towards Mr Dobbs' house, Chrissy

said, "Wow these houses are fantastic, they must be four storeys high.

Fig said, "Oh yes, this is where all the rich people live. Just wait here while I talk to Mr Dobbs."

Fig knocked on Mr Dobbs' door and the butler answered.

"hello Fig i didn't know you were working for Mr Dobbs today."

Fig replied, "I'm not, but I need to speak to him."

"Okay, let me speak to him, wait there," said the butler.

A few minutes later, Mr Dobbs came to the door, with a booming voice he asked

"Hello Fig, what can I do for you?"

"I have some new friends I would like you to meet."// "New friends? Why would I want to meet your new friends?"

Well they are a bit different.

"Well, errr, well," Fig stumbled.

"Come on boy spit it out," shouted Mr Dobbs.

"They are from the future. 1981 to be exact."

"Well in that case, I must meet them, where are these friends of yours?"

Fig beckoned them over. "Mr Dobbs would like to meet you." All the lads walked over to Mr Dobbs. Mr Dobbs was intrigued, "Come in, come in boys, make yourselves comfortable. So, boys, you are from the future?"

"Yes," said Woodsey They all nodded in agreement.

"Can you give me proof of this? I can see you are wearing strange clothes and funny shoes."

"They are called trainers and they are all the style in 1981," said Campbell.

"Okay," said Mr Dobbs, "I need better proof than clothes." Fig said, "Show him your money from the future."

Dobbs said, "That would be interesting."

So Gaffo pulled a £5 note from his pocket and passed it to Mr Dobbs.

"Well this is interesting, 1981 date and who is Queen Elizabeth II? Amazing! Bank of England. I think I believe you, there is no technology around to make such a thing. Can I buy this from you?

"Well, errm, for the right price," Gaffo said.

"I will give you £100 in today's money."

"Seems like a fair offer," said Mayo.

"Yes," said Gaffo.

Mr Dobbs handed the lads £100.

"Tell me what lies ahead in our future?" said

Dobbs. Campbell replied, "You better answer these questions Woodsey. You are the history man."

"Okay Mr Dobbs, what would you like to know?" Dobbs replied, "Tell me something in the near future." Woodsey began... *In January 1760 the seven-year war starts in India and on 25 October 1760 George III ascends to the throne, but the worst wars will be much later in 1914 the Great War later to be called the 1st world war.*

"My- God, let me write this down," said Mr Dobbs.

"It gets even worse, Mr Dobbs. In 1939 the most terrible war of all time takes place, the second world war.

"Who starts these wars?"

"The main instigator was a man called Adolf Hitler, he was the German Fuhrer (leader), Millions died."

"Millions," said Mr Dobbs, "that's unthinkable."

"It gets even worse, Mr Dobbs, Millions of Jewish people died in concentration camps."

"How did they die?"

"They were all sent to gas chambers and gassed, then burnt, the bodies of men, women and children."

Mr Dobbs asked, "Why would they do this?"

"Because Adolf Hitler did not like Jewish people, He wanted a superhuman race, with no disabilities, if anyone had any defects, they were killed at birth."

"This is awful," said Mr Dobbs, "is there any good news?"

"Yes, it does get better, but there always will be wars, I'm afraid."

"I don't know what to say," said Mr Dobbs.

Then from nowhere, "Here," said Campbell, he shows him a strip of pictures from a photobooth of him and his girlfriend.

"Wow, this is astonishing! a picture with colours and not just one picture, four together! what is this, witchcraft?" said Mr Dobbs.

"It's not witchcraft," said Chrissy, "we have moving pictures called movies, where we can watch and listen to people from the past."

"I can't take this all in," said Mr Dobbs.

Chrissy said, "If you are writing it all down, don't forget Red Rum."

"What is Red Rum? said Mr Dobbs.

Mayo explained, "It's a horse that wins the biggest horse race three times, it is called the Grand National."

Woodsey said, "I can give you a horse where you can win your hundred pounds back. On 4 May 1780 Diomed wins the Epsom Derby."

"Thank you," said Dobbs, "I will put a bet on that if I am still here that is.

Mr Dobbs was deep in thought. "What else can you tell me about the future?"

Woodsey replied, "new drugs, I mean medicines are invented to cure many diseases, but there will always be new diseases to fight. New forms of transport are invented to get us to place's quicker. We travel into space, land on the moon in space-ships. Light is invented, without candles. You can talk to people from one side of the world to the other using a telephone."

"Wait, wait, I can't take this all in," said Mr Dobbs, "it's unbelievable. Well, you all must be wanting to try and find your way back home then."

"Can you help us?" asked Mayo.

"I am an inventor, but a time machine is out of my depth. Sorry boys," replied Mr Dobbs.

"That's okay," said Gaffo, "we managed to get ourselves here, maybe we can find our way back."

"I think we should leave Mr Dobbs now said Wood-sey." "Yes," said Fig, "we need to make our way back to the inn. "Thank you Fig for bringing these pleasant men to meet me," said Mr Dobbs, "hope we can all talk again."

"Yes, we will," said Woodsey.

"Hold on," said Gaffo, "this is the heaviest £100 I've ever felt."

"Well it's all coins," said Woodsey, "they don't use paper money for years to come. We best share it out, to take the weight off you." They all started laughing.

As they were leaving, Campbell said, "Shall we get new clothes, so we don't' stand out so much, I don't like it when everyone is staring at us."

"Good idea," said Mayo. Woodsey asked Fig if he knew a good place to buy clothes.

"Yes," said Fig, "I know just the place and he is a friend of Mr Dobbs; he makes all his clothes, it's called Rubens."

"Okay then," said Chrissy, "let's go to Rubens." Just before they arrived at the shop, Gaffo said to Fig, "Make sure we don't get charged too much, this

money has got to last us." Fig started laughing, "You have more money than I've ever seen before."

"He's right," said Woodsey, "we've got the equivalent of £7500 in our time, so we are very rich."

"Still don't want to get ripped off though," said Gaffo.

"Hey, just think, we can rent the best rooms at the ship inn tonight," said Campbell.

Fig replied, "The two best rooms are available, there is the big room with three beds and the room with two beds."

"Sounds better," said Mayo, "my back needs a comfortable bed.

They arrived at Rubens and Fig walks in first.

"Hello Fig, what are you doing here? I haven't any new orders for Mr Dobbs."// "No, it's not for me, it's for my five friends," said Fig.

"Oh okay, said Mr Rubens, "let me see them. Well what funny clothing you lot are wearing!"

"Here we go again," said Chrissy.

Woodsey asked Mr Rubens if he could fit them out with two outfits each, nothing too fancy, just casual.

"Okay, so you want ten outfits in total."

"No," said Gaffo, "make that twelve. Two for Fig as well." Fig replied, "Thank you very much, that means a lot to me." "While you are at it, can you sort three nice dresses for Mel and three for Rose?" said Mayo.

"Okay lover boy," said Chrissy, "nice dresses for your bird." This made everyone laugh.Mr Rubens asked" what? Size are the girls, Ask Mayo "Chrissy answered, He's
the one that's been eyeing them up "shut it you" replied Mayo.Fig stept in, "I think I've got this."They all set off back to the ship inn with the usual glances and stares.

"I am starving," said Mayo.

"We all are," said Chrissy.

"Well at least we can buy the best thing on the menu today," said Woodsey, "what is the best thing on the menu Fig?"

"It's meat pie," Fig replied.

Campbell had a big smile on his face saying, "Mmmm pie," Gaffo started laughing. "Listen to greedy arse! Come on, let's get back to the Ship Inn."

As they were walking back Chrissy asked, "do you think Jacks will show his face again."

"He might do, but we will have to be ready for him," said Campbell.

"Well we coped well last night, but if he brings more men, we will have to move quicker and hurt him more to get shut of him once and for all," said Woodsey.

CHAPTER THREE

As they walked through the door of the Ship Inn, Rose shouted to Fig, "Where have you been? I need you to help serve the food."

"Sorry Mum."

"Yes, sorry Rose, it's our fault, we went to see Mr Dobbs," said Mayo.

"How is Mr Dobbs," asked Rose, "he is such a lovely man."

"He's fine," said Woodsey, "we have good news as well."

"What good news is this?" said Rose.

"We have money and want your best rooms my good lady and six of your delicious meat pies, and make it snappy," said Chrissy.

"Where did you get this money from?

"They traded in an item to Mr Dobbs,and he paid them for it," said Fig.

"How much did he give you boys?

"We need to go somewhere a bit more private," said Woodsey.

So, they all went into the back room and Gaffo asked how much for the best rooms with food for the next week.

"Two shillings will be fine," said Rose.
Gaffo handed Rose a little bag of coins. "Here you can have this."

"I can't take this, it's far too much, it's over what I make in one year."

"You deserve it Rose," said Campbell.
With tears rolling down her face, Rose thanked and hugged all the boys, one by one.
"Well go on," Rose said, while wiping tears from her eyes. "Go and check your rooms out."

Woodsey and Gaffo claimed the twin room and Chrissy, Mayo and Campbell got the triple room, but they were all happy. The beds were not as comfortable as back home, but it was better than sleeping on the floor. Chrissy was testing his bed by pressing his bum up and down on the bed. "My God, this so -called mattress is as flat as a pancake."

"Just watch the fleas don't jump out and bite your arse." Laughed Campbell.

"Do you think so?" said Chrissy.

"Ask Woodsey. You might catch the black death (bring out your dead)," said Mayo.

In the next room, Gaffo and Woodsey were being more serious about what would happen next.

"Do you think we will ever get home?" asked Gaffo.

"To be honest, I don't really know, but we will just have to keep looking and hope we see a sign of some sort,It's a long shot, but we will have to try.

"I hope my family are not too worried about me,"

"I know," said Woodsey, "I was thinking exactly the same thing and I'm sure we all are."

Rose called up the stairs for the boys to come down for food, so they all made their way downstairs and sat at the table.

"This looks lovely," said Campbell, "and smells nice too." Chrissy asked for some wine instead of the muddy looking ale.

Rose said, "You can have what you want boys. I've even took more staff on so Fig and Mel can have a few days off."

"Thanks Mum," said Fig", Mel will be glad to have some time off."

Just as he said that Mel came over to the table and asked, "Any room for one more?"

Mayo stood up straight away and said, "There is room here." All the lads started teasing Mayo.

"Hooo give us a kiss Mel."

Mel laughed it off and gave Mayo a kiss on the cheek. Chrissy said, "I like her Mayo a girl with a sense of humour and beautiful as well."

"Okay then when are we going for the packages," said Campbell.

"What packages?", asked Mel.

"Never you mind," said Mayo, "it's a surprise."

"So, who? is going," said Gaffo, "we can't all go in case Jacks turns up."

"Ok," Campbell said, "me and Mayo will go. The rest of you can wait here."

Fig said, "I'll come with you to make sure you pay the right money and I think you will need help bringing all that stuff back."

"It sounds exciting," said Mel, "I can't wait to see what it is." Campbell, Mayo and Fig made their way to Mr Rubens. Woodsey took a sip of the wine, "Yes, that's better than the ale anyway. I will be drinking this from now on until we leave."

Mel looked sad, "When will that be then?"

"We don't know Mel. Not until our business is finished here, I suppose," said Gaffo.

"I will miss you all when you go,

"Yes, especially Mayo, hey Mel," said Gaffo.

"Shut up!" said Mel, "well, he is handsome."

"I'll get you some spectacles Mel," said Woodsey. They all had a little giggle together.

The Chinese man appeared again and came over to Gaffo. "Nice to see you again," said the man.

"What is your name?" asked Gaffo.

"It's Chan."

"Nice to meet you Chan, I am Gaffo and this is Woodsey."

"They are strange names, where do you come from, I mean what is your origin."

"We live in Liverpool, it's in the North West of England."

"I have been there many years ago, "but how did you achieve such a technique in your fighting skills?"

"From my sensei,"

"I have never seen these moves before."
Woodsey joined in the conversation. "It's a long story Chan. You seem like a nice bloke, maybe we will tell you more about us over the next few days."
Chan said, "Yes of course, maybe we will talk later."
"I'll look forward to it," said Gaffo.

The doors of the inn swung open, "Daaraa!" Mayo walks in with Campbell and Fig behind holding a stack of brown parcels up to their chins.

"Here you go that's yours Chrissy and that's yours Gaffo, there's yours Woodsey and yours Mayo and mine," said Campbell,
"ooow, we have two left," Mel's eyes lit up as Campbell passed her a big brown package.
"Last but not least, the lovely Rose." Rose's face beamed as her and Mel pulled out three lovely dresses each. Rose and Mel were dancing around holding their dresses up. It was no more than what they deserved for their generosity to five strangers from Liverpool.

"Go and try them on then girls."// They both dashed off to their rooms. Ten minutes later they came down both visions of beauty and all the locals were cheering and whistling. They looked so happy.

All the lads went to their rooms and you could hear the laughter coming from both rooms, as they all tried on the clothes. It was a funny sight for them all. Chrissy was running around both rooms with his thumbs in the top of his jacket doing a cockney walk. They were all in fits of laughter except for Fig, he couldn't work out what to make of it all, but he did have a smile on his face.

They all went downstairs to have a drink of wine and enjoy themselves. Gaffo tried to give Rose more money, but she refused to take it, as we had given them so much already.

Meanwhile, Chrissy had a lady of the night sitting on his knee again and looked like he was enjoying himself. Chrissy came over to Woodsey and said,please tell me when "do" they invent toothpaste, Her breath, I can't get past it."

"It's alright Chrissy, I don't think she wants to kiss you, not on the lips anyway," said Campbell.
Woodsey said to Chrissy, "If you can be diplomatic ask her to rinse her mouth out with salt water three times a day.
It's a natural antibacterial remedy.Tell her not to drink it just to gargle."

"Will do Woodsey, cheers for that." And off he went.
Woodsey said to the rest of the lads, "Let's see if Chrissy gets a slap across the face or will she take his advice haha.

Music started up from the corner of the room. It looked like a guitar, but it was a funny shape. Mel grabbed hold of Mayo's hand and said, Let's dance." Mayo was a bit embarrassed, but he couldn't say no, and he didn't mind when she gave him a big kiss on the lips. It was a bit of a strange dance that they were doing, so Gaffo got up and started doing the robot and body popping. You could see the faces on all the locals looking and wondering what's? that dance he is doing, but they all started to clap and cheer, even Chan was clapping with a smile on his face. Then Woodsey and Chrissy started dancing like Madness do, this made the crowd cheer more. Woodsey shouted, "One Step Beyond," Campbell stayed by the bar, as he didn't like dancing. Just to finish off Gaffo started doing the Russian dance, which brought great amusement to everyone. The night was coming to an end and they all went upstairs to their rooms. They were all feeling very tired and it wasn't long before they were all sound asleep.

One mile away Jacks and his men were having a meeting. "I've heard they were all having a lovely time at the Ship Inn tonight, weren't they Smudge?"

"Yes, they were," replied Smudge.

"And look boys, look at the mark they left on Smudge's forehead."

All seven men were looking at Smudge's forehead.

"What is it Jacks," one of them asked.

"It's an imprint of the ring one of them horrible lads were wearing."

Oh yes," said Jacks", not only a ring, but a gold ring with a sovereign coin attached to it, but it says 1937 with George VI head on the coin. Look at Smudge's forehead, it's all there. I knew there was something odd about those boys. The clothes they wear, the shoes they wear and the strange moves they make, I want that ring. it will make us rich. Who's in with me?" All the men cheered.

"Yes Jacks, we are with you," said Smudge.

Jacks set out a plan to attack the boys. He planned to do it outside in the streets away from the Ship Inn, so no regulars would gang up on them.

"Yes," lets attack them in the streets we will have more chance in the open," said Smudge.

CHAPTER FOUR

The next day all the boys were up early having had the best night's sleep for a while. Woodsey and Gaffo were up first.

"My mouth is like sandpaper," said Gaffo.

"Gargle with some salt water, it will make it better," said Woodsey.

"Oh yes that's better." As Gaffo takes another swig to gargle, there is a knock on the door.

"Yoo hoo are you decent?" In came Chrissy (*taking the piss as usual,*) "come on girls, let's get something to eat."

"Okay we're coming now love," said Gaffo.

They all went downstairs to the bar and Rose had set the table for them. Campbell said"Mmm yummy bread and butter again."

"Best be grateful," Mayo said, "many people don't even get to eat in the mornings."

"I know," "I was just kidding *where's your sense of humour gone?"*

Just then Fig and Mel joined them at the table.

"It's strange in here when it is empty," said Campbell.

"It is isn't it. Just us and sawdust on the floor,"

said Woodsey.
Fig suggested that they all go out for the day.
"Yes, that sounds good," said Mayo, "are you coming with us Mel?"
"Yes please," said Mel, that sounds like fun."
"Where shall we go Fig?" asked Chrissy.
"There is a carnival in town with street performers."
"Do you mean fire eaters and jugglers?" said Gaffo.
"Yes, that's right."
"Well I'm up for some of that," said Woodsey, "what time does this carnival start?"
"About 10 o'clock,"
"Well I'm off for a nap," said Chrissy, "I can feel the effects of that wine from last night."
"Go on then you lightweight, the real men will wait here until you are ready," said Gaffo.

It was 9:30 am and Chrissy made his entrance.
"Come on people, what are you waiting for?"
"You, blert," said Mayo.
"What does blert mean?" asked Mel Smiling."
"It means he's an idiot," said Gaffo, "now come on let's go."
Campbell opened the door of the inn. "Come on then, are we going to this carnival? I want to see if there are any clowns." Mayo pointed to Chrissy and said, "we have a clown here." Mel laughed out loud, then everyone started laughing. "Alright, alright," Chrissy said, "lets hit the road."

As they were getting closer to the carnival, Campbell said, "I can feel someone watching us and it can't be our clothes because we look normal. Well, as normal as possible anyway."

"You're just paranoid," said Gaffo, "the streets are packed with people, so I'm not surprised."

"I know there are lot of people around," Campbell said, *but still, he felt uneasy.*

Unknown to the lads, Jacks and his crew of men were hiding in the shadows waiting for a chance to pounce. "When are we going to hit them?" Smudge asked.

"When they least expect it. We will wait until they get more relaxed and then we will catch them off guard. That ring is mine," grinned Jacks.

Mel grabbed Mayo's hand and suggested they watch the puppet show together.

"Okay, but aren't we a bit old for puppet shows?" said Mayo

Mel just laughed. "You're so funny."

Mayo looked blankly at Mel and said, "Well it's been a while since I've watched Punch and Judy."

They took their places and settled down to watch the show. Fig whispered to Woodsey, "he doesn't know what he has let himself in for."

"What do you mean?"

"It's not a children's show, it's about real stories of murders and war, just wait and see."

Halfway through the show, Mayo was getting bored and turned to Mel, "Shall we do something else?"

"Just wait for the good bit. It's coming soon."

No sooner did she say that when one of the puppets hands produced a knife and slit the other puppets throat. There was blood everywhere. Mayo jumped up and said, "This is horrible he walked over to the lads, "Jeez, did you see that? You wouldn't get away with that back home, you'd get locked up."

Everyone was doubled up laughing at Mayo's expression. Mel came running over and said, "You missed the best bit."

"Missed the best bit? you need help Mel."

This made everyone laugh even more. Mayo said, "You're cranks, the lot of yeh."

"Oh look!" Woodsey said, "it's a strong man competition. If anyone can beat the strong man, they win a prize."

"Are you going for it then?" said Chrissy to Woodsey.

"What do you think then lads?"

They all thought it was a good idea, that it wouldn't do any harm. Woodsey said, "I will give it a try," He approached the man and asked what the prize was to beat the strong man. The man mocked Woodsey saying, "You will never beat Big Henry, you little squirt."

To which Woodsey replied, "Oh little squirt is it? well for that, I don't want the prize, in fact I will give five pennies if he beats me."

"You're cock sure of yourself, aren't you?"

"Yes I am. Now get big Henry out and let's get this show on the road," demanded Woodsey.

"My pleasure," the man shouted, "ladies and gentlemen. Gather around for the next victim against Big Henry." The crowd began to cheer and clap. Campbell shouted, "Come on Woodsey, don't be show boating and just get the job done."

A man came up to Campbell and asked what Woodsey's chances were. Campbell told the man that he had a good chance of winning.

"Would you like to put your money where your mouth is boy?" said the man.

"It depends what odds you're giving my friend."

The man replied, "I will give you 20/1."

"Okay, I will put 10 pennies on my friend." They shook hands on it and the man marked his bit of paper.

"Ladies and gentlemen, is everyone ready for the fighting contest with Big Henry against," and the man whispers in Woodsey's ear, "what's your name?"

"Woodsey."

"Against Woodsey." The crowd erupted cheering for Henry. Woodsey was warming up getting himself ready with a bit of shadow boxing, making the usual boxers grunts, as he punched his fists. The crowd found this highly amusing. Then Big Henry stepped out. He wasn't tall, but he was very muscular. Chrissy shouted, "Run Woodsey, Run for your life."

Fig and Mel were very worried, as they had never

seen Big Henry ever lose a fight. They asked Campbell to try and stop the fight. He said, "No way I've got money on my mate." winking at them both.

Meanwhile, Jacks and his men were watching. Smudge said, "This is the perfect opportunity to ambush them, while one of them is being crushed by Big Henry."

"No," said Jacks, "let Big Henry finish him off, then there will be one less to worry about."

"Oh yeah," said Smudge, "that's a good idea."

At the ringside, the man rings the bell, Big Henry runs straight at Woodsey and gets him in a bear hug. You could see Woodsey's face turning purple, as he gasped for breath, Gaffo shouted,"Slam your hands on the side of his head," but Woodsey couldn't hear him.

Mel and Fig looked upset, "He is going to kill him," Mel said.

"It's okay," Campbell said, "he's just playing with him."

Just as Woodsey was at his last breath, he leaned back his head as far as he could and headbutted big Henry right on the bridge of his nose. Big Henry dropped Woodsey to the floor, as he held his nose, there was blood streaming down Big Henry's face, which gave Woodsey time to recover. Woodsey saw his chance to get the upper hand while Big Henry was still reeling in agony, so he threw two hard punches to his rib cage, left and right. This angered Big Henry even more, he took a swipe at Woodsey, but he managed to duck out of the way, but he felt the force of the swinging arms, with the wind rushing past his ears like a hurricane. He thought to himself, if he catches me with one of these blows, I am finished. It was time to finish this fight, as the crowd were getting worked up. Woodsey ran at Big Henry and jumped on him, sending them both to the floor. Woodsey punched him two more times on the bridge of the nose again. That's when big Henry submitted and Woodsey was crowned the winner. The crowd were cheering, as they had never seen a fight like this before. Campbell suddenly noticed the man he had the bet with try to slip away. "Where do you think you're going, Money please or you will end up like Big Henry."

"Yeah, no problem. Here you go." He gave Campbell his winnings.

Jacks was seething, as this had ruined his plans and it made him even more wary of taking on the lads for Mayo's ring.

"I think that's enough excitement for one day," said Gaffo.

"I don't know about that, we haven't seen you dance yet today," said Chrissy.

"Maybe later," "when I get a few beers down me,"replied Gaffo.

Just as they were making their way back to the Ship Inn, they bumped into Mr Dobbs who was with his wife Helena.

"Hello young men and Mel, how are you all?"

"We are fine," said Fig.

"Well how different you all look in your smart new clothes, I see you are spending your money wisely."

"Yes," said Woodsey, "it was much appreciated."

"Oh no problem at all and by the way you put up a great display against Big Henry. Marvellous! Marvellous! wasn't it, Helena?"

"Yes, it was," she replied. Mr Dobbs asked if they would all like to come around for another visit, so they could talk more. Everyone agreed and Helena offered to make dinner and make a day of it. Helena suggested they should come the next day. The lads were happy with that.

On the way back Fig suggested a short cut down an alleyway, which would take ten minutes off the journey.

"Come on then," said Mayo, I'm hungry now after watching Woodsey getting his arse kicked."

"Hey watch it," said Woodsey.

Chrissy stopped suddenly, "Did you hear that?"

"Hear what?" said Campbell.

Chrissy was sure he heard a noise, then a voice came from a dark doorway. "So, you think you can make a fool out of old Jacks, do you?"

Then Jacks appeared but with more men at his side and they were all brandishing knives.

Chrissy shoved Fig and Mel in the middle and Chrissy,Campbell, Mayo, Gaffo and Woodsey made a circle around Fig and Mel, facing Jacks and his men.

Jacks said, “I want that gold ring. Give it to me and you can all go without any harm and I won’t give you any trouble again."

“Don’t believe anything he says,” said Mel.

“Be quiet, stupid girl.”

It was all getting a bit tense, as this was quite a dangerous situation.

“Just give me the ring,” snarled Jacks.

“No,” said Mayo,” it’s precious to me.”

Jacks was furious, “Right, we will just have to take it then.

“Come on then try it,” said Chrissy.

One of the men lunged at Mayo and caught the top of his arm, but Mayo caught the man with a punch to the face, which dazed the man, but Mayo was injured. Campbell saw a stone on the floor, so picked it up and threw it at another one of the men and it hit him on the side of his head, sending him reeling to the floor. Gaffo realised he had to get to Jacks and maybe the rest of them would back off. He made a move to attack Jacks but was met by two men standing in front of him. The only thing he could think of was to disarm the men and throw them to his mates to deal with and that is what he did. He easily disarmed the men and pushed them to the circle, where Woodsey and Chrissy dealt with them with ease. Gaffo came face to face with Jacks, but more men with knives came to Jacks aid.

Gaffo shouted, “I need a weapon to deal with this.” Then from the back of Jacks men a long wooden

pole came over the top of them. Gaffo caught it and said, "That will do nicely."
This was just the thing he needed. As he started striking out, he knew he had the upper hand, as he was easily disarming any man that tried to attack him. Jacks tried to leave, because he knew it was all going against him, but he was met by Mr Chan and Henry.

"Where do you think you are going?"
The rest of the men scattered, fearing for their lives, but Jacks wasn't so lucky. Henry grabbed him and pinned him up against the wall.

"Put me down Henry, "said Jacks.

"No," said Henry, "why did you attack these young men?"

"It's got nothing to do with you. Just put me down, please Henry," pleaded Jacks.
The lads were wondering why Big Henry was helping them, especially after the match with Woodsey.
Mr Chan stepped forward and said, "Hello boys. Henry is my friend, and I noticed these men following
you from the carnival, so I asked Henry for his help and he was happy to."

"Why would he be happy to help us?" said Woodsey.

"Because he respects you all, the way you fight with courage and the way you protected your friends Fig and Mel against these horrible men," explained Mr Chan.

Henry still had Jacks up against the wall with his feet dangling in mid-air.

"So, Jacks are you going to be a good boy and stop bothering these young men?"

"Yes," said Jacks, "I will stay away, I promise."

"I don't want you to go near the Ship Inn ever again or I will crush you," warned Henry.

Henry lowered Jacks to the floor, and he ran off like a scurrying rat.

Gaffo said to Mr Chan, "So it was you who gave me the wooden pole."

"Yes," said Mr Chan, "I knew it would help you in this situation."

"Thank you so much," said Campbell, "but why did you help us?"

"That's another story, can we go back to the Ship Inn and I will tell you everything, but it will have to be in private, I don't want any unwanted ears listening in."

"Okay," said Woodsey, "we will have to get Mayo's wound looked at as well."

They all arrived at the Ship Inn and Rose noticed Mayo's injury straight away.

"What's happened here, who would want to harm you?"

"It was Jacks and his men, they all had knives," said Campbell.

"Get him upstairs to his room and I will dress the wound."

They all made their way upstairs. Rose was curious, why was big Henry here with the Chinese man. Woodsey explained to Rose that they were friends and they helped them, after he had beat Henry in a fight. Rose was confused, but Woodsey explained they would soon find out why they were here.

Once they were all in the room, Rose and Mel cleaned Mayo's wound.

"So, Mr Chan," said Gaffo.

"Please, just call me Chan."

"Okay Chan, what is it you want to tell us all?"

"Do you want to discuss it in front of Rose, Mel and Fig? because I know about you and I have been watching you all since you first got here,"

"I knew it! said Campbell, "I felt someone watching us since day one."

"Yes, you were right," said Chrissy, "after we thought you were paranoid."

"I don't get it," said Rose, "what is all the secrecy?"

"I think we need to let Rose and Mel know how we got here it only seems fair." They all agreed with Woodsey.

"So, Fig," said Rose, "you seem to already know what's going on,"

"Sorry Mum, I promised everyone I would keep it a secret."

"That's fine," said Rose.

"So Chan, can you explain to us all what it is you have to tell us," asked Woodsey.

"Yes," said Chan, this is going to sound strange."

"I think we've had a lot of strange things happening to us the last couple of days," said Campbell// "Okay, I will try to explain the best way I can. You are all here because of me." The lads all looked at each other.// "I summoned you here to help me find my daughter, she was kidnapped a week ago by the Shia, who are very dangerous and evil and will stop at nothing to get what they want."

"Why would they take your daughter- and what do you mean, you summoned us here?" said Mayo.

My daughter has very special powers, which the Shia want to exploit for their own means. I have powers, but not as strong as my daughter."

"Okay, okay, stop there," said Woodsey, "your daughter has special powers, and you have powers, so how did we get here?"

Chan said, "Please, just let me explain. I made a spell for someone to help me and all of you were sent to this place and I have followed you since you appeared on the street from that mist."

"Why us and why someone from over 200 years in the future," said Campbell.

Rose and Mel looked puzzled and looked at each other.

"I thought you were different," said Rose.

"So, we were chosen somehow to help you get your daughter back," said Woodsey.

"Yes," said Chan," I was surprised when I first saw you all, because you are so young. That's why I followed you, to see why it was you lot that were chosen and as I got to know you over the last few days, I was convinced by your fighting skills, your respect to your friends and you all seem to have good morals, which I feel comfortable with, so do you think you could rescue my daughter?"

"Sure," said Gaffo, "but do you promise to send us back home when we get your daughter back."

"That goes without saying," said Chan.

"Yes!" said Chrissy", we are going home! I can't wait to eat crisps and drink coke again!"

"It's not going to be easy, as we are dealing with very dangerous people."// "No problem Chan, we can take them," said Chrissy.

"We will need weapons," said Chan,

"What kind of weapons? asked Gaffo.

"Powerful ones," said Chan.

Campbell asked Chan if he could get gunpowder, coconuts and some fuse wire. Chan was curious, so Campbell illustrated how he could hollow out the coconut, fill it with gunpowder, place fuse wire into the coconut and it would explode, and the shell splinters would cause injury to the enemy. Chan was taken aback by the idea but was not sure where he could get coconuts. Campbell suggested if he couldn't get coconuts that anything with a hard casing would do. Woodsey asked Chan if he knew where his daughter was. *The Shia had a hide-out on the Isle of Wight and that is where they had taken her*.

"We are going to need a ship and crew to get to the Isle of Wight," said Campbell.

"I will provide all the weapons, the ship and the

crew," said Chan.
"Can you use your powers against these people?" asked the lads.
Chan replied, "Yes I can, but not until I have the location of where they have my daughter."
"We are having dinner with Mr Dobbs and his wife Helena tomorrow. I'm sure we could ask him if he has anything which could help us rescue your daughter," said Woodsey.
"That would be great," said Chan, "can we all meet again tomorrow night to discuss where we are going next? "Okay," said Gaffo, "tomorrow it is then."

They all went downstairs for a drink and something to eat. Mel was amazed by the story but was also upset because she knew that they were all eventually going back home, especially Mayo. She grabbed his hand and said, "I don't want you to go, but I know you have to."
Mayo hugged Mel and gave her a kiss. "I love you Mel." And the biggest smile came across Mel's face. Rose poured wine for the lads. The music played and the singing and dancing began. Henry held Rose by the hand and said, "Dance with me." Rose accepted. She asked him if he was married. Henry told her no I am single and you could see the instant connection. After the dance Henry told Rose that he would never let Jacks near the Ship Inn again. Rose looked very happy.

Chrissy sat down with Woodsey, Gaffo and Campbell, while Mayo danced with Mel. Fig was

helping his mum behind the bar.
Chrissy said, “Do you think we can help Chan get his daughter back?”
Gaffo replied, “If we are the ones his spell chose to bring to him, then I guess we can, but it won’t be easy because these people, the Shia, sound like the mafia of our day, but with more power and mystery behind them.”
Woodsey leant forward, “as Gaffo said it chose us “now don’t ask me why, but it did and it doesn’t matter if we were in Dovecot park or a main road like East Prescot Road, it would have happened anyway, so we need to do this for Chan and then we are on our way home.”

“I can’t wait,” said Campbell," as much as I like Rose, Fig and Mel, “it will be nice to get home.”
Mayo joined them and they explained to him what they were discussing. He agreed with them, he would be glad to get back home, although he would miss Mel and would like to take her with them, he knew it would be impossible.

“We need to get some rest tonight, we have to go to Mr Dobbs’ for dinner then I think Chan will need us to go through the plans to what happens next,” said Woodsey.

“I know,” said Mayo, “why don’t we invite Chan to come along to Mr Dobbs’, I’m sure we met Mr Dobbs for a reason and he is an inventor, so he may have ideas that would be useful for Chan."

“Yes, why not,” said Woodsey, “it’s worth a try, I think we need to rest now, it’s going to be a big day tomorrow."

They all got up to go upstairs when Chan walked over to them, "Goodnight boys, we will meet tomorrow to work out our plans.

"Yes," said Chrissy," we have just been discussing that it would be a good idea to join us for dinner at Mr Dobbs' house tomorrow, because he may be able to help with him being an inventor.

"If he doesn't mind, that would be great," said Chan, "I will see you all tomorrow." Then Chan went home.

"I am knackered," said Woodsey.

"That must be the kicking you got from Big Henry," said Chrissy.

"Alright, but I did win, and Campbell made a few bob from it."

"Yes, I did indeed," said Campbell, "and I need to spend it before we go home."

"I would keep some if I were you, they will be worth a few quid back home," said Woodsey.

"Okay, I will keep some then and buy some new clobber with the money I make."

As they were walking upstairs, Woodsey started singing, "Mama is a jetsetter, Daddy likes to fly away, Mama got a red letter, the day her Daddy passed away, Mama lives in Sweden, Dad lives in Spain, they fight for my attention, but I can see through their game.

They all joined in the chorus, "They are Trans-parents, I can see through them, they are Trans-parents, a million miles between them."

Mel and Fig didn't know what to make of it, as the song was not recognisable to them. It was called Trans-parents by a Liverpool band called Afraid of Mice. The lads would go and see the band perform when they used to sneak to the Bow and Arrow pub and try not to get kicked out.

"Right then lads that's enough singing now I am getting my head down for the night," said Woodsey. Everyone was tired, so they agreed to meet at 8:30 am for breakfast, on Chrissy's watch anyway.

Morning came and Campbell was the first up again, with his morning fart.

"My God Campbell, I can't wait until I get my own room back home, away from your smelly arse."

Campbell chuckled to himself and said, "I can't wait for a decent bog to sit on."

"No wonder Woodsey and Gaffo went in the other room, the rest of us didn't get a chance, crafty gets." Said Mayo.

Just then Gaffo knocked on the door. "Are you ready yet? me and Woodsey will see you downstairs."

They all sat down for breakfast and Mel and Fig joined them. "Morning everyone," said Mel, they all said morning back to her.

Fig seemed quiet, Chrissy asked him if he was okay.

"No, not really, I would really like to go with you to help rescue Chan's daughter."

"It will be better that you stay here with Mel and

your mum. Things will get very dangerous, and to be honest, you will get hurt if we are not able to save you from harm," said Gaffo.

"I know," said Fig, "I understand, but I will miss you lot when you go back to Liverpool, to your future. It won't be the same around here."

Rose came over and gave Fig a hug. "Don't be sad Fig, you and your sister have played a big part in this adventure." "That's right," said Mayo, "we wouldn't have met Mr Dobbs without you, you have played a big part and Chan will thank you for that."

Fig was happy to have been a help to the lads and Fig had a big smile on his face, as he hugged Mel.

After breakfast some of the customers started to come in, so the lads decided to stay in their rooms until the afternoon, then make their way to Mr Dobbs' house for dinner and hopefully he would be able to help with their quest to rescue Chan's daughter.

A couple of hours went by and everyone was having a snooze. Rose knocked on the door. "Hello boys, are you awake? Chan has just arrived,"

"Okay Rose, we are coming now," said Woodsey. "Wow, I needed that kip, Now I am ready for dinner."

"Hello Chan" said the lads as they walked into the bar.

"Hello boys, are you all ready?"

"Oh yes," said Chrissy, "I could eat the back off a giraffe." This brought a smile to Chans face, "Well you must be hungry then, but I haven't heard that saying before, that's quite funny, eat the back off a giraffe' hahaha."

"Shall we make our way then?" said Fig.

"Yes, thank you Fig," said Chan, "please do show us the way."

"I've asked Henry to watch over the Inn while we are all out in case Jacks goes back on his word."

"I don't think Jacks will ever come near this place again especially now Henry has the hots for Rose," said Campbell. Rose heard this and looked embarrassed, "Go on you lot get out and go and have your posh dinner with Mr Dobbs."

They all laughed, "Oooow," said Chrissy, "I think we touched a nerve there."

Fig interrupted, "Come on, let's go, Helena will have the food ready."

They all arrived at Mr Dobbs' and Fig knocked on the door. The butler answered. "Hello Fig, Mr Dobbs is expecting you all, please come in."

They were all shown into the dining room and there was Mr Dobbs and Helena sitting at the head of the table. "Hello everyone," said Mr Dobbs.

Fig asked Mr Dobbs if it was okay for Chan to have dinner with them. "Of course, any friend of yours is a friend of mine."

"This is lovely, I haven't tasted anything like this for a while," said Fig.

"Thank you, Fig," said Helena, "I did have some input in the kitchen, it wasn't all my cook's doing."

"Yes, it is delicious," said Chan, "thank you for having me."

"Not a problem," said Mr Dobbs, "here have a taste of the wine, I think it will be to your liking."
Chan tasted the wine, which was very nice and thanked Mr Dobbs.

"Mr Dobbs, we need to tell you how we got here," said Woodsey.

"So, you know how you got here?"

"Yes, but I will let Chan explain it to you."
"Thank you," said Chan, "I used a spell to bring them all here."

"A spell?" Gasped Mr Dobbs. "And how did you do that and most importantly- why did you do it?"
"The reason I cast the spell was that I needed help."
Mr Dobbs asked, "What help did you need so badly that you had to bring these boys from over two hundred years in the future?"
Chan explained, "As you may have guessed, I have powers to do such a thing and my daughter Mia has powers far outreaching mine and this is where the problem lies. you see, Mia has been kidnapped. I am sure she has been taken by a group of people called the Shia."

"I am sorry to hear that," Mr Dobbs said, "you must be very worried, who are these people?"
Mr Chan replied, "They are very bad people from China, they are why I left China with my daughter, to try and keep her safe, but they caught up with us and they took Mia."

"Do you know where they are keeping her?" said Mr Dobbs.

"Yes, the advantage is, I can locate Mia wherever she is."

"That's amazing," said Mr Dobbs "and how do you do it."

"Okay," explained Chan, "I will show you all, I need a candle." Helena passed a candle to Chan.

"Thank you," said Chan, "can everyone look at the wick of the candle."

They all looked at the wick of the candle, which suddenly lit by itself. There were gasps of amazement from everyone and this was just the start. The next thing, above the candlelight appeared images of Chan's daughter Mia.

"My God," said Gaffo, "it's like a projection from a cine camera."

"What is a cine camera?" asked a startled Mr Dobbs.

"It's what we have back home with moving pictures, and we have television sets we can watch moving and talking images on."

Mr Dobbs was writing all this down.

They all carried on watching the images from the candle, it wasn't good to watch as they witnessed Mia being dragged away. Chan explained that the images were his memory of what he saw. They all watched in disbelief seeing Mia scared and crying. It was very upsetting, and they could see the anguish on Chan's face. Chan pointed out. "You can see the ship with black and white sails that Mia was taken on." They all nodded in agreement. "I will take you to the latest image I have of Mia." Suddenly there was Mia tied up and gagged.

"Where is she?" asked Mr Dobbs.

"It's the Isle of Wight. I saw it when they took Mia ashore."

"I have good friends on the Isle of Wight," said Mr Dobbs, "they may be able to help you."

Chan told Mr Dobbs, that these were very dangerous people and that he wouldn't want anyone to get hurt. That is why he cast a spell for help and these five brave young men were sent to him. Mr
Dobbs agreed with Chan that these lads certainly knew how to handle themselves and were very nice young men.

Chrissy said, "We want to help out, it's what we do, we are Scousers." All the lads started laughing, but not everyone knew what Chrissy meant.

Chan was getting weak and the images started to fade. Helena went over to Chan and gave him a hug and said, "We will help you whatever you need, me and my husband will help."

"Thank you," said Chan," I am very grateful to you both." Campbell asked Mr Dobbs if he could get any coconuts.

Mr Dobbs didn't think he could and wanted to know what he wanted them for. Chrissy explained how he could make bombs by hollowing the coconut out, filling it with gunpowder, put a fuse wire in the powder, when it exploded the

shell parts act as a bomb from the explosion. Mr Dobbs asked if he could hollow balls of glass in the same way.
Campbells- eyes lit up. “Balls of glass? That’s perfect! Don’t forget to leave a hole so I can fill them with gunpowder.”
“I think I’ve got that” said Mr Dobbs.

Chan began to gather his strength. *It was amazing the power he had, that he could pinpoint where they were holding Mia that would make it much easier to find her.* Chan explained that most of what they saw today was Mia’s power. She was the one conducting through him and she could do that at any time. Mia goes into a dream state and would have been able to see all of them today in that
room. “That’s impressive,” said Mayo, “so she knows we are coming to help her.”
“Yes, she not only can see you, she would have heard everything as well.”
“This is good,” said Gaffo, “she can let us know how many we will have to face and what weapons they have.”
“Mia has already done that There are three men with her at all times in the room. Mia is locked in and there are six men guarding the building around the clock. Now, these are not only people who are in Shia, they are scattered all over the world There may be only nine men guarding Mia now, but they are highly skilled Ninjas It will be a tough task to get her back.”

“Nine- Ninjas, let me at them. It’s going to be fun!” said Gaffo.

“What’s the next move then Chan?” asked Chrissy.

Chan replied, “I do have a plan, I have a ship and it's ready in two days.

“I still can’t believe that we five were chosen for this task,” said Chrissy, “I’m still pinching myself to see if I’m dreaming.” “Believe me, it is not a dream and we will be heading for the Isle of Wight in two days.”

Chrissy patted Chan on the shoulder and said, “Bring it on, I’ve always wanted to knock a Ninja out.”

This brought a big smile to Chan’s face and he said, “And this is the reason you were all chosen, you are all very brave and I couldn’t have asked for a better group of people, thank you.”

“Hear, hear,” Shouted Mr Dobbs. “I couldn’t have put it better myself.”

Mr Dobbs raised his glass. “Here’s to the safe rescue of Mia.”

“Yes,” said Chrissy," I will drink to that."

Mr Dobbs took Chan to one side as the rest sat drinking with Helena. “Exactly what kind of power does Mia have? I mean- I don’t mean to pry.”

“That’s all right,” said Chan, “you are an honest and kind man and I think you deserve to know. Mia has more power than she knows herself, it has run through our family for centuries, but Mia has shown that she is more powerful than anyone has

seen before. Mia was moving objects when she was six months old, so this has brought unwanted attention from the Shia Especially Chi their leader."
"What does this Chi want with her?"

"He wants to control her and use her as a weapon for his own needs and not for good deeds. But what the Shia don't understand is, it could all blow up in their faces.
This power needs to be controlled," explained Chan.

"How old is Mia."

"Fourteen. As she gets older, the power will grow stronger."

"I would like to meet her when she gets back."

"I am sure you will, as you and your wife were meant to be part of all this, just as much as the boys are."
Mr Dobbs came over to Campbell and said, "I will have to get to work making the glass balls for you."
"Nice one Mr Dobbs," said Campbell.
Woodsey thanked Helena and Mr Dobbs for the lovely Dinner Evening and kind hospitality shown to them all.
Chan agreed and said it was time he left to get the final part of the plan together. They all decided to leave together, so Mr Dobbs could continue with his work.

CHAPTER FIVE

Mia was sitting tied to a chair; three men stood close to her watching her facial expressions closely, as instructed by Chi. He had explained to his men that if there are any odd movements or her eyes begin to roll, they must call him straight away. Mia would never show this when she contacted her father. She would simply close her eyes as if she were asleep and her eyes would roll under her eyelids and then she could make contact, like she had done this night. She could see her father and all who sat around the table at Mr Dobbs' house. This made her feel happy, as she knew help was on its way, but she couldn't let it show that she was happy, as this would alert Chi. He could work out what she was seeing, and this might put her father and anyone who tried to help her in danger.

Chi would come into the room to test Mia every day. He would ask her questions like. You look happy today, is someone coming to help you. Is it today or tomorrow? He would ask these questions every day, but Mia would never let her emotions show and this frustrated Chi. When he left the room, he would kick and punch everything or anyone that was near him. He was unable to read her, so he couldn't see what was coming.

Mia was scared, but knowing help was coming made her feel better inside. The guards would never speak to her, they wore masks and were fully clothed in black. All Mia could see were their eyes. They were only small in stature, but they moved very quickly. One would sleep from time to time, but there was always one awake at all times. The same as the men outside, two would rest and four would stay awake at all times. Chi was a control freak, and he was determined to control Mia's powers for his own benefit. Chi had plans to start a slow water torture on Mia to see if he could crack her. He was hoping this would finally break her, so she would finally show some kind of expression.

Back at the Ship Inn, all the lads were having a drink and Chrissy was mixing with the ladies of the night, Again. He gave his favourite girl a kiss and put his thumb up to Woodsey. Woodsey started laughing, "I take it the salt water is working for the bad breath then."

Gaffo, Mayo, Campbell, Fig and Mel burst out laughing.

"What did you make of Chans home movie today?" said Gaffo.

"I know, it was mad wasn't it?" said Woodsey.

Campbell said, "Nine Ninjas. It's not going to be

easy. I know we can handle ourselves, but Ninjas, that's a different ball game."

Gaffo interrupted Campbell, "Look I probably know more advanced moves than them so that will be to our advantage."

"It is for you," said Mayo, "but what do we do when they run at us with silly little kicks?"

"Well you hit the nail on the head," said Gaffo, "most of their moves will be kicks." Gaffo stood up and told Mayo to kick him.

"What do you want me to kick you for?"

"I just want to show you all a simple move, which will help you."

Mayo stood up and kicked out at Gaffo, who grabbed his foot and walked backwards quickly, which caused Mayo to fall to the floor. "Now that will help you all when the time comes." Mayo got up from the floor and wiped himself down, "I will definitely use that move."

Mel said to Mayo, "You are my hero, and you will all be successful in bringing Mia back." Then she gave him a kiss.

Woodsey looked at Campbell, Gaffo and Mayo and said, "We all know it's not going to be easy, but if we were chosen, then we must give it our best shot."

"Of course," came the reply from the lads.

"Now let's get drunk," said Gaffo.

Chrissy came over to the table and said, "I've just been outside with that bird and I...

"Whoa!, hold on a minute! I would rather not know," said Campbell.

"Keep it to yourself there is a young lady present."

"Sorry," said Chrissy," errrm, I will tell you later Mayo."

Mel laughed. "Don't worry about me I have seen it all working here."

Fig came over to sit with them. "So, what's going on tonight then?"

"Ask Chrissy," said Mel.

"Haha!" Gaffo laughed. "I like you Mel, you have a wicked sense of humour."

"I see Big Henry is in again," said Woodsey.

"Yes," said Mel, "he is a lovely man and mum is very fond of him and the best thing is, Jacks is terrified of him."

"It's a win- win situation then," said Woodsey.

Fig asked Campbell if he could see the pictures of him and his girlfriend again, so Campbell got them out of his pocket and handed them to Fig. "She is beautiful with white hair."

"That's not white, it is called blonde and she dyes it," said Chrissy.

"Shut it you," said Campbell, "its natural"

Fig didn't know what they were talking about, as he walked off gazing at the pictures and showing them to the customers. You could see the look on their faces of disbelief. The lads knew they were safe, everyone liked them, the way they handled Jacks.

The music started up again in the corner and everyone started clapping and shouting for Gaffo to start dancing. It didn't take long before he was up doing his body popping and Russian dance moves. The customers started shouting. "Sing!"
So Woodsey, Mayo, Chrissy and Campbell started singing the Beatles song.'Twist and Shout.' Woodsey started it off, 'Come-on, come-on, come-on baby now!" and the lads joined in.
'Come-on baby'
Woodsey, 'Twist and Shout'
the lads, 'Twist and Shout'
The locals loved it but didn't understand the strange songs these five boys from Liverpool kept singing.

They all sat down for a rest and Rose brought them some wine over. "Here you go boys, drink up You lot have brought me more business since you arrived and with Jacks out of the picture, more punters are coming through the doors."
"Don't forget Henry," said Chrissy.
Rose smiled and said. "Don't be cheeky, you."
"I'm off to bed," said Campbell.
"The place is still bouncing," said Chrissy, "so I'm staying up a bit longer."
"You're just after Betty bad breath over there," said Gaffo.
"No, I'm not," said Chrissy, "and anyway, she hasn't got bad breath anymore, and Woodsey, she has passed your tip on to the rest of the girls."

"Glad to be of assistance" Grinned Woodsey. "one more day and we're off on a big wooden ship, so I'm going to bed."
One by one they all left the bar to get some rest.
Finally, they were all asleep. It was about 2:30 am when Mayo sat up in bed and he could see Mia in the middle of the room. She spoke to Mayo, "Quick, wake up your friends."
Mayo shook Campbell and Chrissy, "Wake up! wake up!
"What is it?" said Chrissy.
Campbell wiped his eyes.
Mayo said, "Look it's Mia. She wants to tell us something. I will go and get Woodsey and Gaffo."
Mayo ran next door and burst into the room. Gaffo and Woodsey shot out of bed.
"What's? going on," said Woodsey.
"It's Mia."
"What about Mia?" said Gaffo.
"She's next door. She wants to tell us something."
"Is Chan here?" said Gaffo."
"No. Just come quickly."
The three of them rushed next door and were shocked to see Mia standing in the middle of the room, like a hologram, flickering. Woodsey said to Mia, "What is it you want us to know?"
Mia spoke, "firstly i know where you are all from and I appreciate what you are all doing for me. I am being tortured at this very moment."
"Are you in pain Mia?" they asked.
"No. I let my mind leave my body and my face

shows no expression, which is what Chi is looking for."

"Is he the leader of the Shia?" asked Woodsey.

"Yes, he is, and he is very angry that he has found no answers yet."

"Why is he torturing you and what are they doing to you?" asked Campbell.

"It is water torture, where a drip of water hits your forehead for hours on end and he wants to find expressions on my face, so he can see what's happening in the future, but I am not showing any signs on my face."

"Well isn't that a good thing that they can't read you?" said Mayo.

"Yes, it is, but Chi is losing patience with me. I can read his mind and going on what he is thinking, I have one day left."

"Have you contacted your father?" asked Woodsey.

"No, I don't want to, not like this, but could you let him know as soon as possible."

Then the picture began to fade. Mia was getting weak, she had to stop before Chi began to notice. Then Mia vanished.

"We need to let Chan know what's going on," said Woodsey. Campbell stood up and went to Fig's room. "Fig!" Campbell shouts.

Fig came to the door yawning. "what's up?"

"We need to get hold of Chan right now. We've just had a message from Mia, and we need to tell Chan what she said."

“Right,” said Fig," I will go straight away.” And off Fig ran. Fifteen minutes later Fig returned with Chan; they were both out of breath.

“What is it?” said Chan.

“Mia appeared to us tonight,” said Mayo, “she needs our help sooner rather than later.”

“It must be serious if she appeared to all of you tonight, so we need to act now,” Chan demanded. *Chrissy asked Chan if the ship was ready for them. It was, but he was short on crew and they would have to improvise*

.

On the way down the dark streets going towards the docks Woodsey notice a group of men. He went over to them and asked if they needed work. They all did need work and then Woodsey realised it was Jacks's men and walked away.

“Please....” one of them pleaded, we are desperate and hungry."

“But you are Jacks's men," replied Woodsey.

“I know, but we have no quarrel with you anymore Even Jacks has respect for you lot.”

“Okay,” said Woodsey, “are you prepared to fight for us to rescue a young girl.”

They all nodded their heads in agreement.

“Okay, we are going to be up against a lot of men dressed in black and they are all very quick. Instead of trying to fight them face to face, how good are you at throwing knives?”

Then a figure appeared from the shadows and it was Jacks himself.

Chrissy came over. "What does he want? We have no time for him."

"Please hear me out," said Jacks, "we are all cold and hungry and we will do anything to help."

"What makes you think we can trust you?" asked Chrissy.

"I give you my word," said Jacks, hitting his chest with his fist.

"I don't know," said Woodsey.

"I understand why you don't trust us, but I promise we won't turn on you again," said Jacks.

Woodsey discussed the situation with his friends, they did need all the help they could get with the crew and fighting and had no time to find other men, so they decided to give them a chance. Gaffo wasn't convinced but told them all he would keep a close eye on them.

Woodsey went over to Jacks and his men. "Okay you're in, but any wrong moves and you and your men will be going overboard."

"Thank you," said Jacks.

"Well don't thank me yet, you will be working as crew and there may be trouble."

"Yes, my men have told me about the men in black."

"Okay, how good are your men at throwing knives? because you can't fight these men face to face, so you will need good aim."

"I think we can manage that."

"Okay, you will all get fed as soon as we get aboard, I will give you 100 pennies to share

amongst yourselves."
Jacks and his men looked happy that they had some purpose and were being paid as well.

The lads carried on walking towards the ship with Chan, Jacks and his men followed behind them. Chan said, "well who would have thought we would all be working together."

"Maybe this is part of the plan," said Campbell.

"You could be right," said Chan.

As they got to the ship Gaffo could see Fig there. "What's Fig doing here?"
Then he noticed Mr Dobbs was also with him. Chan told Jacks to report to the head crewman, who would give them food and tell them what duties they would have to do.
Gaffo went over to Fig and Mr Dobbs, "You got here quick, didn't you?"

"Yes, Fig came to tell me you were heading here to leave early, so I brought Campbell his special bombs."

"I think he will like them." Gaffo shouted, "Campbell! Come over here and check these out!"
Mr Dobbs opened the wooden case and pulled out perfectly round glass balls full of gunpowder with a fuse wire attached. "Wow! That's perfect," said Campbell.

"Well, have fun," said Mr Dobbs.
Then he left with Fig. Fig looked back and waved. You could see the sadness in his eyes, but the lads knew they would see him again.

"Right, let's go," said Chan," we need to set

sail, we don't have much time."
The ship began to move, and Campbell was looking over the port side, then Chrissy joined him. "I bet you never thought we would ever get to sail on a wooden ship."

"No," said Campbell, "it's like a dream and I think we are going to experience things we have never seen before."

"A lot more," said Chrissy, "what about Jacks and his men? I bet you never thought they would be helping us. "I will keep an eye on them, but as Woodsey said, we can throw them overboard if they start any trouble."

Woodsey and Gaffo approached Jacks as he worked on deck.

"Jacks we need a word," said Woodsey.

"No problem," replied Jacks.

Gaffo "asked Jacks again on how good was his throwing skill with knives"

"Good, I think," said Jacks. He took a knife from Gaffo and threw it, but the handle hits the target and falls to the floor.

"That's not good enough," said Gaffo with a long sigh. Go and round up your men."

Jacks went off to gather his men.

Gaffo looked at Woodsey shaking his head, "I will have to give them some lessons in knife throwing they will be no use to us when the fighting starts."

"What do you think about Jacks?" said Woodsey.

Gaffo replied, "I think he is dejected by the way we have beaten him twice and he has lost credibility with the locals, which they hold no fear, you can see he is lost, but this will be to our advantage."

"Why do you think that?" asked Woodsey.

Gaffo replied, "We can teach him skills and encourage him and his men, we will have them eating out of our hands."

Mayo walked up to join Woodsey and Gaffo. "What's happening?"

"We are going to teach Jacks and his men some knife throwing skills," said Gaffo.

"Well as long as they don't throw any at me, I've already been on the end of one of their knives," said Mayo.

"Don't worry," said Gaffo, "they were all at a very low point on the docks, now they have a purpose, and they are getting paid."

Jacks and his men turned up and showed Gaffo their knives.

"Not bad," said Gaffo, "now let's see if you can hit that mast."

Smudge stepped up first and threw his knife and it just bounced off the post.

"No, not like that," said Gaffo, "you don't hold the handle when you throw, put the blade between your finger and your thumb."

Smudge looked at Gaffo, with a strange look. "Won't that cut my thumb?"

"No, now watch this."

Gaffo threw the knife at the post with the blade between his thumb and finger and it dug straight into the post.

Jacks and his men were amazed by the accuracy of Gaffo's throw, so they were all eager to have a go. Gaffo gave Smudge his knife back and he threw it at the post, but it fell out because it wasn't deep enough.

"Try again," Gaffo said.

He tried again and the same thing happened.

"That's good, but you will have to throw harder, keep practising."

Chrissy and Campbell came over. "What's all the commotion?"

"Just getting them to practise throwing knives for when the action starts," said Gaffo.

Gaffo got the men to make a line and take turns to throw." Have ten throws each, then get back to work, as we don't have much time on our hands."

The lads left them to it and went to talk to Chan.

Smudge turned to Jacks as they lined up for practise. "What do you make of these people and what's our plan" "Our plan?" said Jacks, "our plan is to do what these people ask us to do."

Smudge looked bewildered. "What do you mean Jacks." "Don't you realise they are giving us a chance," said Jacks, "after everything we have done to them. That's never happened to us before and I respect them and admire them. Maybe if I'd treated people better in the past, we would have got on better and still had a roof over our heads, instead I've been horrible and that's going to change, if we manage to make it back."

"Do you think we may not make it back?"

"Yes, there is a good chance of that," said Jacks, but if we do get back, we will go back very different people."

The lads were sitting with Chan discussing what approach they were going to take, when they reached their destination. *Mia had shown Chan the site where she was being held and night- time would be the best time to hit them.*

"Yes" Gaffo butted in. "Night- time is best, but ninjas are very well trained, so not very much gets past them."

Chan explained, "We'll be okay docking the ship, but we'll have to go by foot to where Mia is being held and it's quite secluded."

"That's better than I thought then because we can spread out and hit them from all corners," said Woodsey.

"We still need to go in quietly," said Gaffo, "so we can take a few out before it all kicks off."

"When can I start bombing them?" said Campbell.

"Here we go,,You can't wait can you?" said Chrissy, "You're a friggin fire bug."

Mayo chirped in, "I want a go of those bombs too."

"Well you two can carry them," said Chrissy.

Chan stood up and said. "I'm going to get some rest and I think you should all do the same."

"I agree," said Woodsey, "we're going to have to be fit tomorrow."

And they all went to their beds to get some rest.

Mia was still being water tortured by Chi, and he was getting angrier with Mia. He told his men to stop and then he took a towel and wiped Mia's face and head.

Mia didn't like this, as she wasn't expecting it and Chi saw a reaction for the first time, because after he dried her,

he noticed tiny beads of sweat on Mia's forehead. Chi started to laugh and clap his hands, and this made Mia lose control of her concentration even more.

"I can see haha!" he said. "He is coming for you, isn't he? your father, Chan, I know he is! So, Mia, are you going to show me some of your powers?"

"Why do you want me?" said Mia.

"Because with you, I can defeat all who come before me and I will have everything I've ever wanted."

"I won't do anything for you," Cried Mia.

"Oh, but you will, because when your father comes for you, we will capture him and torture him until you show me what you are capable of." And with that Chi left the room to talk with his men.

Mia went into a trance, so she could hear what was being said. She could hear Chi telling his men *to hire*

pirates to check the ships approaching the island and kill all the crew but bring Chan back alive.

Chan was sitting up on his bed when Mia appeared

before him. "Mia I've been so worried, what's happened?"

"I am so sorry Father, but they know you are coming."

"It's okay my child, don't worry, we'll be okay."

"But Father, they said they are going to kill everyone except you, they want you so that they can make me help them in their quest and if I don't, they said you will get hurt."

"That is not going to happen, trust me Mia. I have five very brave young men with me and we have some extra men to help us now, so everything is going to be alright and I know he is not going to hurt you now because he is concentrating on capturing me. Just let him try."

Mia had a slight smile on her face as she faded, and Chan knew that this would be the last message until they rescued her.

Chan knew their plans had to change and trouble was coming earlier than expected. Chan sat on his bed contemplating his next move. He was feeling drained with not being able to sleep worrying about Mia. Woodsey knocked on Chan's door "Chan, we are just having something to eat, will you join us?"

"Yes," said Chan, "I will be with you soon."

All the lads were eating bread at the table. Chrissy was biting at the hard crust, "arrgh! I can't wait until I can have egg on toast again with plenty of melted butter on it." licking his lips at

the thought of it.
"Shut it you," said Mayo, "you are only making it worse by speaking about it."
Chan came into the room with a tired sad looking face.
"What's the matter?" said Gaffo, "you look awful."
"Sorry about that," said Campbell, "diplomacy was never his strong point."
"No, he is right," said Chan." Mia appeared to me last night." All the lads stopped eating and were listening intently. Chan continued to tell them that Mia gave him news that the Shia knew they were on the way to try and rescue her and they have sent pirate ships to stop them ever reaching the island.
"My God," said Mayo, "this is bad news. Not only taking them on land, but at sea as well."
Chan nodded, "Yes it's made things more difficult for us all. Their plan is to kill all of you and keep me alive, so they can use me to get Mia to use her powers against their enemies. So, I have come to a decision, to send you all home, so nobody gets hurt."

Close by Jacks was listening in on the conversation and he barged in the room,"no", we can't turn back! this is giving us a purpose in life for the first time. Me and my men are willing to try whatever the outcome. We have been looked down upon for as long as I can remember, maybe if we do something good then more people will give us

a second chance like these young men have."
Chrissy stood up, "I'm with Jacks on this one."
Gaffo said, "I think Chrissy speaks for us all. We are going to get Mia back for you."
They all agreed that there was no going back. Chan was pleased, but concerned as well "Thank you," he said, "thank you all."
Gaffo went over to Jacks and patted him on the shoulder. "Nice words, now let's get some more practise with knife skills, you are going to need them against these pirates." "Don't worry about pirates," said Jacks," I know most of them and they know me. The thing with pirates is, you can buy them if you have enough money."

Chan heard this and said, "This is interesting, so do you think they will work for us against the Shia?"

"Well," said Jacks, "let me talk to them first and maybe they will not attack, but I don't' think they will fight with us."

"Okay, but what if we pay them not attack us and just sail away and not work for the Shia?" asked chan.

"That could work," said Jacks, "lets, just see what happens when they arrive."
Gaffo asked Jacks to get his men together for more practise and they both went on deck.
Chrissy said, "I don't know, but can we really trust pirates? I can feel Jacks passion and you can see he is up for it, but pirates?"

"I don't know," Campbell said, "but Jacks is

friends with them."

"I don't think he is friends with them," said Woodsey,' maybe just acquaintances. We'll have to tread carefully."

"Bombs at the ready." said Campbell.

"That's a good idea," said Mayo.

Chan was taking all this in and said, "For such young men, you all know what you're talking about."

"Well, we have over two hundred years of experience and we have watched a lot of pirate movies and they are all depicted as backstabbing bastards," said Chrissy.

"I see what you mean," said Chan.

Chan asked what weapons of the future would be useful for them now. Woodsey jumped in," where shall we start? Machine guns would be helpful."

"What is a machine gun?" asked Chan.

"It is a gun that fires rapidly up to five bullets a second, that's all we would need to take out all the ninjas and rescue Mia."

"That's amazing," said Chan, "are there bombs like what Campbell has?"

"That's nothing compared to what has been invented," said Campbell.

"What kind of bombs have been invented?" asked Chan.

"All kinds of missiles and bombs," said Woodsey, "Bombs that can blow up a whole ship in one hit."

"My goodness," said Chan.

"That's not all," Woodsey continued, "the worst bomb to ever have been used is the atomic bomb, which was dropped on Hiroshima and Nagasaki in Japan. This happens on 6 August 1945 at the end of world war II. This bomb, being so powerful it wiped out both cities and not many people survived. Chan was very upset hearing this news and held his head in his hands for quite some time. Mayo went up to Chan and put his hand on his shoulder "Come on we have Mia to think about now, so let's put all our energy into rescuing her."
"Yes, yes. You are good boys," said Chan.
Gaffo was going through a few techniques with knife throwing and they were all getting better.
"Well done. You're all improving. Keep it going."
You could see they were all enjoying the practise and it felt like solidarity was forming. Campbell and Mayo were looking over the side of the ship.
"Where are we?" said Mayo.

"I think we are on the English Channel," said Campbell.

"What makes you think it is the English Channel?" said Mayo.

"Because it's rough," With that Campbell spewed up vomit everywhere.
All the crew started clapping and cheering. Jacks said, "I was wondering when the first of you would be sick."
Mayo replied, "No chance of me being sick, I've crossed the Irish sea may times."
Jacks came up to Campbell, "Never mind lad, some

of the toughest people I know get seasick."
This came as no consolation to Campbell, as he belted out another pile of sick.

"Put some salt water on the sick before he smells it," said Jacks.

"I need water," said Campbell. Mayo passed him a jug.

"There you go, get that down your neck." Campbell swigged it down quickly.

"Thanks Mayo, he said. As he wiped tears from his eyes. Chrissy walked over. "Come on you tart let's sort where these bombs are going."
Campbell got his bearings and looked around the ship for the best place to store the bombs.

They decided to plant ten at each end of the ship and ten at both middle sides. This would give them the advantage, whichever way attacking ships would approach. Chan had his chart out; he was trying to work out what time they would reach the island. Woodsey asked if they would reach it by night-time. *It would probably be the next evening, which would give them more time to work out a strategy*. Chan knew they wouldn't hurt Mia while they were hunting him, which gave them time.

Nightfall was approaching and all the lads were still working out tactics. Gaffo asked Jacks how many of the pirates he knew. *Jacks knew quite a few of them.* Chrissy wanted to know who was the one to be careful of. Jacks named Carlos.

He would be the one to double cross them out of them all, the rest were predictable. *If they made a deal with them at sea, they would be on their way.* Jacks would call out Carlos's name when he approached, so they could identify him and be ready for him.

The crew were all settling down for the night. Jacks's men broke the rum out. Chrissy was straight over. "Let's have a try of that please."

"Be my guest," said Smudge. Chrissy took a swig and liked it, it was tasty, so he passed it around then they all nodded in approval. One of the crew started playing a squeeze box and singing a shanty song. Chrissy started doing a silly dance, which made the crew laugh loudly.

"These young men are mad," said Jacks.

"We are always up for a good party and a sing song," said Gaffo.

"What songs do you sing?" asked Jacks.

"You wouldn't know the songs we know," said Mayo.

"Give us a melody and our men will soon join in with you." Campbell shouted over to Woodsey. "Come on give us a song."

Woodsey replied, "They couldn't play along to the songs I sing."

All the crew joined in, "Come on, let's hear a song."

"Okay, okay, let me think of one. This is a song called Beautiful View' written by a song writer from Liverpool called Phil Jones. Woodsey begins to sing. "There's a beautiful view outside my door,

I don't go out there no not anymore, there's a pair of wings in the bottom drawer, I don't use them, I don't fly anymore.
Music plays (squeeze box). 'All this beauty has no meaning, without you to share with me, all this beauty has no meaning without you to share with me. There are many places across the sea, I'll never go there until you go with me. There are many songs I have never
sung; I'll never sing them until you sing with me. All this beauty has no meaning, without you to share with me, all this beauty has no meaning, without you to share with me."
Woodsey finishes the song and all the crew clap and cheer. Jacks shakes Woodsey's hand. "I like that song; I would like to sing that myself."
"Sure, you can," said Woodsey, "but don't copy-right it." Jacks looked puzzled, but just smiled.

Chan reminded everyone to keep their wits about them and not to get drunk, as they could be taken by surprise. They all agreed that two men would have to keep watch. They worked out a rota of two hourly switch overs enabling every-one to have a turn to keep a look out and get some sleep.

The night passed over without any prob-lems and everyone got up early. Chrissy looked rough.
"My God Chrissy," said Mayo, "you look like a bag of shite."
"Quite an improvement," said Campbell.

"Haha, very funny you all are. Nothing a curer won't take care of," and he took a big swig from the rum bottle, "Arrrr!That's lovely."
Jacks looked at Mayo, "Can I just say I'm sorry about what happened to you when we ambushed you."
Mayo replied, "well I'm sure we all will forgive you, when we bring Chan's daughter back."
Jacks put his hand out and shook hands with Mayo saying, "It's a deal. By the way why as your gold ring got that date on it?"
Mayo just looked at Jacks, "Because we are from the future." Mayo walked off to find Campbell, leaving Jacks looking baffled, scratching his head. Mayo walked over to Campbell, "Are we ready for the worst then?"

"Oh yes," said Campbell, "I hope they don't make a deal with us, so I can blow their ship to pieces."
Mayo smiled. "You just can't help yourself, can you.'

"Well what's the point of having these beautiful works of art if we are not going to use them?"

A cry came from the crew "Ship ahoy!". Chan rushed out of his cabin. "Right men, stand at your stations and don't engage in battle until I say so."
The ship was drawing closer. Chrissy shouted. "It has skull and crossbones, it's pirates alright!" Campbell grabbed a torch; he was itching to light up his first bomb. The pirate ship was getting close and the pirates had their swords drawn. Jacks

stood at the side of the ship. A man appeared with a very long beard and pot belly.

"Walrus!" shouted Jacks. "Jacks! What are you doing here?" Everyone eased slightly.

Jacks called over. "I am helping my friends rescue a young girl."

Walrus replied, "Sorry, but we are being paid by the people holding her, so it looks like you are in trouble, my old friend."

"Can we come to some arrangement?" asked Jacks. "Maybe double the money you have been offered?"

Walrus stroked his beard, "I suppose we could, but what would we have to do for your money?"

"You could help us rescue the girl."

"No, we can't do that. Only a madman would go against the Shia."

"Okay," said Jacks, "what about if you sailed on to your next venture?"

"How much are you offering?" asked Walrus.

Gaffo pulled a bag of money out and threw it up and down in the palm of his hand.

Walrus licked his lips. "I think we can do a deal," with a grisly laugh, "so why don't you throw that money over here?"

Gaffo looked at Chan. Chan nodded his head and just as he went to throw the money a big booming voice came from the pirate ship. "Do you think you can buy yourself out of this mess Jacks?"

"Carlos!" shouted Jacks.

"Yes, it's me and you are all going to die!"

Carlos was tall with long black hair with a short stubble beard.
Chan shouted. "Right men- don't hold back."
The pirates started jumping on to Chan's ship, but some
didn't quite make it and hit the side of the ship, which sent them to their deaths. The men started to fight, one to one combat sword fighting and men punching each other. Woodsey and Mayo were ducking out of the way of swooshing swords and managing to punch the men with precise boxing style. Gaffo took men out with his martial arts skills. Chrissy was with Jacks' men who were handling themselves very well. Carlos was annoyed by the fact things were going against them. Chan threw
Gaffo a wooden pole once again. Gaffo jumped on to a higher level and men were swiping their swords at him, He jumped up and the swords just swiped under his feet, this then gave him time to hit them with the pole. More men came aboard, Chan joined in the fighting and showed some amazing martial arts skills himself. Campbell lit the first bomb and threw it on to the pirate ship. Seconds later,"' Boom,"' There was an almighty blast, which not only tore a massive hole in the side of the ship, it also left men scattered all over the deck. Carlos was shocked by what he saw. He had never seen anything like it before and he knew then, there was only going to be one winner.
"Retreat! retreat men!" Shouted Carlos.

"Not so quick," Screamed Campbell. He lit another bomb and threw it on to the pirate ship. All the pirates dived for cover, as they now knew how deadly this weapon was.'"Boom'" Another blast. All you could see were bits of timber flying up in the air. The pirate ship slowly drifted away, a large fire had started, and all the sails burned down. You could see Walrus, Carlos and what was left of his men trying to put the fire out, but things didn't look good for the pirates, as their ship drifted off aimlessly in a cloud of smoke.

A big cheer came from the crew, but Chan knew the tougher task lay ahead this very day, but at least the men were in good spirits. "Right," said Chan," we need a head count."

Amazingly no one was killed and only two men had small cuts from knifes.

"We need to throw these bodies overboard," said Chan.

The crew gathered all the dead, twenty -one in all, and just as they prepared to throw them overboard Woodsey said, "Wait just let me say a short prayer for them all."

Jacks said. "Why? They have just tried to kill us."

Woodsey replied, "I will pray for their souls, not what they were in life."

"Okay," Jacks said, "do what you have to do."

Woodsey bowed his head said a private prayer in silence and made the sign of the cross.

"Okay, you can lash them in now."

Chrissy burst out laughing. You could hear splashing as the bodies fell into the sea. Chan also thought this was quite funny, as he didn't follow any religion.

Gaffo approached Chan. "Nice moves, you kept that quiet didn't you."

"Well it's always good to add an element of surprise."

"Quite right," said Gaffo.

Jacks shouted over to Campbell. "What the hell were they you threw at that ship?"

Campbell replied, "My exploding beauties and by the looks of things, they could win us any battle."

Chrissy, Mayo, Woodsey and Gaffo went over to Campbell, "In your element there weren't you?"

"Oh yes," said Campbell, "did you see the look on Carlos's face when the first one went off?"

"What do you think now though about people dying?" said Woodsey.

Chrissy interrupted" what do you mean? it was them or us and they were just arseholes."

"Yes," said Mayo, "they had the chance to walk away or sail away and I won't be losing sleep over them anytime soon." "Just asking," said Woodsey, to see where your heads are at."

Chan rang the bell. "Listen everyone, we will be hitting land in about two hours, so the working crew will stay and man the ship, me and these five young men will be going on land along with Jacks and his men, so that's thirteen of us all together."

"Unlucky for some," said Chrissy.

Chan finished off by thanking everyone for their

help.
Chrissy asked Campbell what? was the score with the bombs. Campbell explained that it was a bit tricky, if they are thrown too early, they can be thrown back at them. If held for too long, they can explode and blow up everyone in close- proximity. The best way to use them is light the fuse wire count to five and throw It will explode about two seconds after. Chrissy thought for a moment and said, “I think I will leave it to you, I will probably blow myself up.”

A cry came from one of the crew. “Land ahoy!” You could just make it out like a shadow in the distance. Chan shouted to the crew, “Okay men-- you know where we are docking- it's in your hands now.”

CHAPTER SIX

Chi was taunting Mia, "Not long now, your father will be here soon and then you can show me what you are capable of. My pirate friends will have killed all his men by now and will be heading back with your father at this very moment."
A single tear ran down Mia's face because she was unable to see for herself what had gone on. This made Chi very- happy as he thought this emotion of sadness was to his advantage.

"This has been so easy," said Chi "and I will enjoy torturing him, if you don't help me."
A few hours had passed and there was no sign of the pirates' return with Chan. Chi started to grow increasingly agitated. He could not understand why it was taking so long. He threatened to stab Mia through the heart-, if they didn't arrive soon. Mia kept calm and just looked at the floor.

Chan's ship eventually made land. It was quiet where they docked, enabling them to keep a low profile. Chan recognised the path that Mia had shown him when she first appeared to him, it was ten minutes away. Two of Jacks men were carry-

ing the bombs in a wooden crate. Campbell said, "Don't drop them. They might blow up."
The two men put the crate down and refused to pick it up again. Chan reassured them they had to be lit before they would explode, and that Campbell was just
messing around with them. Chan pleaded with Campbell for no more joking, they did not have the time.
Campbell apologised and the two men picked up the crate with a nervous look on their faces.

As they drew closer Chan said, "We will have to be as quiet as possible, we are not far from them now."
Chrissy whispered, "I can see a faint light in the distance." The night was drawing in, so it made it easier to see where they were keeping Mia.

"It will be best if we surround the house," said Woodsey. Chan told Jacks and his men to go to the back of the house and he would stay at the front with the five lads.

"Okay," said Jacks lets go men."

"Remember, don't let them get too close and put your knives to good use," said Gaffo.

The house was made of wood and was two storeys high, but there was no light coming from the top floor. Campbell whispered to Chrissy "I can see three ninjas, just about, they are dressed in black, but when the light is behind them you can see them, I don't want to use the bombs yet, it will put Mia in danger."

Chi was getting upset. "Where are they? They should have been back by now."
Mia could sense something, but she wasn't sure if her father was captured or if he was safe. Chi went outside to see if anyone was approaching the house. He shouted to his men, to go and look to see if
anyone was coming. This was perfect for Chan, as they could take them out without alerting Chi. Chi slammed the door as he went back in. Two Ninjas stepped forward and left the front of the house. Chan said to Gaffo, "We can take these two."

"Okay," replied Gaffo.

All the lads and Chan were crouched down behind bushes. The Ninjas were getting closer to them. Chan looked at Gaffo and they both jumped up at the same time, Gaffo grabbed one from behind and put his arm across his throat until he collapsed. Chan jumped on top of the other one and got him to the ground. Chan tried to cover the Ninjas mouth, but it was a struggle. The Ninja managed to cry out. Woodsey came to help Chan and punched the Ninja on the bridge of his nose, which knocked him out. They then tied them up and gagged them.
Back at the house the other two Ninjas heard the cry and went inside to warn Chi that they were under attack. This made the situation worse. Mia

smiled to herself, as this confirmed that her father was ok, and he was here to help. "What are you smiling at girl?" shouted Chi. "Do you think you are safe now? I will show you." Chi picked up a sword and went to drive it into Mia, but it deflected off her. Chi couldn't believe it, it was like Mia had a forcefield around her, which was impregnable. Chi was shocked but amazed by the power Mia was showing.

"At last," Chi said, "now you show your powers, impressive. Very impressive." Chi ordered the rest of the Ninjas to go outside and eliminate the enemy

and bring back Chan's head, while he was laughing to himself.

The last seven Ninjas left the house to carry out Chi's orders. As soon as they left the building they were met by Jacks and his men. Jacks shouted." Come on you sorry excuses for men!"

The Ninjas came at the men jumping high in the air and kicked out at the men. One of Jacks men took a full blow to the head, which knocked him out. Smudge threw his knife, which caught one Ninja at the top of his arm-making it harder for him to fight. Four Ninjas attacked Chan and the lads. Gaffo was at the front, he called out. "Okay let's see what you've got!"

One Ninja came at Gaffo kicking and punching in a fast motion. Gaffo managed to block all his punches, but took a kick to his ribcage, which hurt him, causing him to fall to the floor. While Gaffo was down the Ninja pulled out his sword and was just about to stab when then a knife flew- through the air and stuck in the ninja's neck. Gaffo looked to see where this knife had come from and he could see Jacks standing with a smile on his face. Mayo and Chrissy took Gaffo's advice by grabbing the Ninjas kicking feet and pulled two of them to the ground by walking backwards. Jacks men took advantage of this and beat them up while they were on the ground. Woodsey and Campbell took a few blows by the fast-moving Ninjas, but they managed to get a few punches in. Chan could see he and his friends

We are getting the upper hand, as the Ninjas started to retreat. Five Ninjas were still standing and were all in front of the house. These Ninjas are very proud- men and don't take defeat lightly. Plus, Chi does not like it when he doesn't get what he wants. Campbell shouted, "I'm fed up with these jumping little shits!" He threw a bomb at the front of the house. ' BOOM', a big explosion erupted, then a cloud of smoke and all you could see were the last remaining Ninjas on the floor and a massive hole in the front of the house.

Suddenly, Mia appeared walking slowly. Chan called out to her "Mia. My child! Come quickly!" But just following behind her was Chi. He swung his sword once again towards Mia, but again it just bounced off her, like it was hitting a stone. Everyone was expecting the sword to cut right through

her, they all gasped when the sword deflected off her. They all realised Mia had remarkable powers. Chi knew he had been defeated and made a run at Chan, so he could take revenge. He didn't get anywhere near Chan, as Jacks and his men stood in his way and killed him in seconds.
Chan thanked everyone as he hugged Mia He said, "I couldn't have done it without you all, I nearly gave up, but you kept me going."
Woodsey said to Campbell, "With the powers Mia has it's not going to stop anytime soon, people will be tracking them all of the time, until her last days."
Campbell nodded, "I know, but at least we did our bit."
Chan said, "Come on then, let's get ourselves back to the ship."

They all started to walk back, discussing what had just happened and how powerful Mia was.
Gaffo walked over to Jacks," Thank you, Jacks, I owe you one."
"Your welcome," said Jacks, "glad to be of service."
They all survived the fight, except for a few small stab wounds and cuts, which wasn't too bad.
"Nice knife skills," Chrissy said to Smudge and the rest of Jacks men. They were all quite pleased with themselves. Chrissy congratulated them all again and told them they should be proud of what they did back there.

Chan was holding Mia close. He was just so glad to have her back. “I will never let anyone take you away again.”
" It’s okay Father, it will never happen again not anymore.” Chan was surprised by Mia’s reply, but he knew she had grown even stronger.
All the lads were walking together.

“Well,” said Chrissy, “I guess we are on our way back home.”

“Yes,” said Woodsey," I can’t wait to see my family again,”

“Me too,” said Campbell.

Gaffo said, “Just think, we will all be eating toast with melted butter.”

“Stop it,” said Mayo, “I’m starving.”
Woodsey went over the Chan, “Is everything okay Chan? “Yes, thank you, Mia is fine, and she appreciates everything you all did for her.”

“No problem, it was our pleasure.”
Chrissy was the first with some of the men to head towards the ship. He noticed something was wrong.

“Look!” he shouted, “more pirates and they are right by our ship!”
Chan ran to the front, “Oh no! My crew. What has happened?”
Campbell called out, “Let me through.” And two of Jacks's men were right behind him with the crate of bombs.
Chan said, “Wait... I don’t want any of my crew put in any danger.”

Chrissy feared that they might be too late. They all got to the dock alongside the ship when two men appeared. It was Walrus and Carlos; they had been rescued by another pirate ship who were also working for the Shia.

"Well, well, look who's here," said Carlos, "I bet you thought you'd seen the last of us, but that was your mistake." Campbell stepped forward, "Listen arsehole, get off our ship and we will let you live."

"I don't think so," said Walrus, "we have all your crew tied up, so if you try anything with them exploding balls, they will all die."

Chan shouted, "No that's not going to happen, I know you are not getting paid by Chi now, because he is dead and so are most of his men."

"You have been busy, haven't you?" said Carlos. "You are correct You have killed Chi, which leaves us
out of pocket, so we need to come to some agreement."

"What's your price?" said Woodsey.

"Well, that bag of money you were prepared to pay us off with will be a start and that gold ring your friend is wearing." "No," said Woodsey, "you can have the money, but not the gold ring."

Mayo said, "The money alone is a good offer, and your employer is dead, so take it or leave it."

"Chi isn't the only one who is paying us, and the Shia is bigger than you think," said Carlos.

Jacks whispered to Chan that he didn't trust Carlos. Chan didn't either. Carlos was getting twitchy, he grabbed one of the crew and put a knife to his throat. "I've had enough of you lot; who do you think you are?"

Just as he finished his sentence a knife flew-through the air and hit Carlos at the top of his shoulder. He let out a scream and let go of the crew member. None of the pirates retaliated, they were more in shock at what had happened.

Gaffo put his hand on Woodsey's shoulder to whisper something to him, but his hand became stuck and a bright light shone from the two of them. Chrissy, Mayo and Campbell saw what was happening and thought, this is it, we are going back home. They all ran over to join Woodsey and Gaffo. Chrissy said, "We can't go now, what about Chan and Mia?"

Chan shouted, "You must join- together, it is time now." Everyone, including the pirates, were all looking at this light and were bemused by it.

Campbell, Chrissy and Mayo all joined Gaffo and Woodsey and they all started spinning around and were elevated above the ship, but it just didn't seem right, it wasn't the same as before. They descended onto the deck of the ship, the light was still glowing, and the pirates looked terrified. Suddenly, the light vanished, and the lads just stood there wondering what was happening. The pirates got a bit braver and started to attack them. Jacks and his men climbed on to the side of the ship, knowing that the lads were outnumbered. But what happened next stunned everyone, especially the lads themselves, there must have been forty pirates surrounding the lads with daggers and swords. Chan thought the worst and could not bear to watch. Jacks's men made it on to the deck while all the pirates were preoccupied with the lads.

Jacks shouted, “So it takes all you lot to take on five boys, a brave lot you are.”

Jacks knew he and his men had a fight on their hands, but he could not let the lads face forty men on their own. Jacks got the attention of at least ten pirates and a brawl broke out amongst them. Campbell was the first to come face to face with a couple of pirates, but he noticed he could move much quicker and he felt stronger. As the pirates jabbed their swords towards him, he ducked and weaved out of the way, then he jumped, but he went ten feet high, came down and landed on top of two pirates. As this was happening all the rest of the lads noticed they all could do the same thing. They all had lightning fast reflexes and super - human strength. Chan couldn’t believe his eyes at what was happening, the lads were all running about at super speed and were throwing all the pirates overboard. Jacks and his men just stood back and watched while the lads finished off each and- every one of the pirates. Chan asked Mia whether she was responsible for giving the lads these powers. No i had nothing to do with it.

“This is very strange,” said Chan, “But I like it”, with a smile on his face.

Jacks and his men untied all the crew, and Chan and Mia came aboard.
"Come on men, let's go back to London."
The crew all cheered and thanked the lads for saving their lives. The lads went over to Chan. "So, what happened there?" said Mayo.
Chan shook his head. "I don't know."
Mia said, "It wasn't me who gave you those powers. My father made a spell to find help to rescue me and you five were chosen and now I know why. I have been watching you all since you arrived and my father was unsure at first, as you are all younger than he thought would come to help, But what I've seen of you all only confirms what I thought. When I was told how you all stood up for your new friends at the Ship Inn on the first day of meeting them. You are five very- true and loyal friends who love and look out for each other. Thats why you were chosen and now the spell has awarded you great powers, which should only be used when necessary and not to taken lightly."
The lads were taken aback by Mia's words. Chan took Mia to his cabin for some much-needed rest.

They could make a movie about us all now, called The Five Super Scousers. Imagine winning the shot putt at the school games. The lads were chatting about what they could achieve with their powers.
"I don't think we will be able to show off these powers, it will bring too much attention," said Gaffo.

"I don't think we will have them when we get back to Liverpool," said Woodsey.

The crew got the ship going. Jacks came over to the lads. "Well you lot can sure handle yourselves even better now, no one is going to mess with you lads again."

"By the way, who threw the knife at Carlos?" asked Woodsey.

"That was Smudge," said Jacks.

"It was a good shot, you saved that man's life," said Chrissy," Shaking Smudge's hand.

Everyone had had enough excitement for one day and headed off to bed, as the lads were settling down Campbell let out a loud fart.

"Arrrgh." said Chrissy, "that was the loudest one yet."

"Yes," said Mayo, "that was your first super-human fart." They all had a good laugh after such a stressful day.

Gaffo woke up first and went out on deck. Chan and Mia were already up and were staring over the side of the ship. "Morning," said Gaffo.

Chan replied, "Morning."

Mia looked deep in thought like in a state of trance. Mia came around. She looked worried.

Chan asked Mia, "What did you see?"

"It's the Shia, she replied, "they are sending their most powerful warlock to try to capture me."

"That can't happen," said Gaffo.

"This doesn't concern you anymore," said Mia,

"my father made a promise, and we are going to stick by it. When we get back to London, we will send you all back home."

"I think I can speak for myself and my friends that we will stay until you are safe from this warlock," said Gaffo.

"No", said Chan, "you have all done enough already and we thank you for that, so when we get back, I will reverse the spell that brought you here."

Gaffo went back to tell the lads that Chan was sending them back home, but they needed to stay until they were both safe. They were all in agreement that they should stay and help Chan and Mia. Chan thought it would be a good idea to let the lads stay. Himself and Mia made the decision to see it through with the help of the lads, they did need them.

The lads wondered if they had been given the new strengths to take on the warlock. Mia didn't know why they were given these powers, but the warlock was a very dangerous man, who would stop at nothing to get what he wanted.

They had heard all this before,they were told Chi and the Ninjas would kill anyone who tried to free Mia and they had won that battle. The warlock would not use weapons or any men to attack them, it would be done by wizardry, which can get out of control and things can become very unpredictable.

"This is all new to us," said Campbell, "even

though we are from 200 years in the future, all this doesn't exist. Wizards and warlocks are stuff of fantasy."

Mia shook her head, "You say it's stuff of fantasy, but it will always exist, whoever is in charge of the country, whether it's Kings and Queens or governments. The warlocks and wizards are always in the background, pulling the strings, now and in 200 years-time

"I knew it," said Woodsey, "I always said there was a higher power behind the government."

"When will we reach London?" asked Chrissy.

"It will be another full day," said Chan.

"That's good," said Campbell, "I can't stand ships."

Just then his face turned white and he ran out to spew over the side of the ship. You could hear a big cheer from the crew as Campbell was heaving over the side.

Gaffo announced to everyone that Jacks and his men should be rewarded for showing such loyalty and saving his life. They all agreed that they had showed a lot of balls when it came to the fighting and they risked their lives to help them, when only a few days previously they had tried to ambush them!

"What do you think we should give them/" said Mayo.

"We have plenty of money left, so I suppose we could give them half of what we have left," said Gaffo.

He pulled out a couple of bags of money.

Chan's eyes widened, "Do you know how much you are giving them?"

"I think so," said Gaffo.

"Well let me just tell you that's a man's wage for about 2 years."

Campbell came back in the room with his eyes streaming and wiping his mouth, "That's better."

"We are going to give Jacks and his men half of the money we have left," said Woodsey. Campbell just nodded in agreement.

They all went on to the deck and called Jacks and his men over.

"What is it?" asked Jacks.

Gaffo handed the two bags of money over to him and said, "I know we are not back in London yet, but here is payment for all your help."

Jacks said, "Thank you, but that's too much."

"No, it's not too much," said Gaffo," you all helped so much, and you saved my life."

"Thank you," said Jacks He sat down with his men and shared out the money.

They all seemed really happy, but most of all they were glad that they had made a difference.

Gaffo said, "I will put in a good word with Rose, to let you drink in the Ship Inn again."

"Thanks," said Jacks, "I would like that."

"But you had better behave yourselves."

"Don't worry, we will," said Jacks, "especially with Big Henry around."

Mayo laughed. "Oh yes, don't mess with Big Henry,

he kicked Woodsey's arse, good and proper.
"As I said before, I actually won that fight and Campbell earned a few quid out of it," replied Woodsey.
"I did indeed," muttered Campbell.
"You didn't share it though, did you, you, minge-bag,"Chrissy muttered.

CHAPTER SEVEN

The English Channel was getting a bit rough and stuff was flying off the tables.

"All hands- on deck, "was the cry.

They all went out to see if they could help. Mia and Chan stayed in their cabin Mia was having a vision. She projected the image on the cabin wall. They could see a very large ship with oriental markings on it and right at the stern was a large figure of a man in a long flowing cloak.

"Is this the Warlock?" asked Chan.

"Yes Father, warlocks don't normally work or associate with the Shia as they have their own agenda with power, so I'm not sure why he's joining them in this quest."

Chan replied, "Why would he help them out? It doesn't make sense at all."

The image faded and Mia sat down. "Father, I wish I was born without this gift."

"I know my love, but it has run through our family for centuries and you are the strongest that's ever been."

"That's what I am afraid of," said Mia, "and if I am backed into corner again, it could be the end for everyone."

"What do you mean, everyone?" asked Chan.

"I have seen a prophecy and it's not good. If my power is used to full effect it will be catastrophic." Chan looked worried, "But why a warlock? it doesn't make sense."

Woodsey and Campbell had just finished helping the crew and the waters became much calmer.

"Have you tried jumping to see how high you can get?" said Campbell.

"I don't think we should," said Woodsey, "it might frighten the crew."

"Go on," said Campbell, "what's the use of having powers if you can't have a bit of fun with them?"

So Woodsey jumped just a little, but his feet went 6ft off the deck of the ship. Campbell tried it, but he jumped higher and ended up near the crow's nest. Everyone could hear him laughing as he came down. Woodsey looked at him and thought what the hell and made a big leap upwards. The pair of them couldn't stop laughing as they passed each other going up and down. Gaffo came out to see what all the noise was, then he saw all the crew staring at Woodsey and Campbell flying- through the air.

"What are you pair of quilts doing?"

"Come on Gaffo," said Campbell, "it's great!"

"No thanks, my stomach has bounced around enough today with this ship."

The next thing was Mayo and Chrissy came flying- through the air.

"Come on Gaffo you knob join in with us!" said Chrissy. Gaffo just smiled and thought,' well if you can't beat them, join them and there they were all flying around like trapeze artists.
Everyone was watching them. Jacks said to his men, "you don't see this every day."
Smudge said to Jacks, "how did you know?"
"How did I know what?" Jacks looked puzzled.
"We joined them to help find the girl, which was dangerous by itself, We fought against pirates that you knew, and we have been paid a year's wage each, so how did you know this would happen?"
"That's the thing," said Jacks, "I didn't know, I just thought it was the right thing to do for once in my life and it's paid off and I like the way I am feeling right now."
"I am with you on that," said Smudge.
The lads were still flying about and doing somersaults in mid-air.
"This is great this! I hope we can still do this when we get back to Liverpool!" said Campbell.
Chrissy started laughing. "Imagine going into school and doing the high jump or the triple jump."
"Yeah," said Mayo, I've never been any good at the high jump."
They all came back down to the deck.
"I'm starving," said Campbell.
"You're always starving greedy arse, said Chrissy."
"It must be all the exercise we're doing."

Chan and Mia came out of their cabin. Chan addressed the crew. “We will be back soon so you will all be able to go to your homes. I would just like to thank you all for everything you have done.”
The crew gave a big cheer. The crew were not fighting men, but they had been through a lot, so it was a great relief for them to get back to their loved ones.

As the ship headed on to the Thames river, you could hear the noise of the docks as all the ships were unloading cargo. Woodsey said, “This is what it must have been like on the Mersey Docks.”
“There are a lot of strong smells coming from these ships,” said Gaffo.
“They come from all over the world, Food, tea, minerals, all kinds of stuff,” said Woodsey.
Finally, they docked, and the ship was anchored. Chan would take Mia home for a rest and would meet up with them the next day. Jacks and his men needed a well-earned drink after the stressful few days they had just been through. Gaffo asked them to come to the Ship Inn.
“Are you sure?” replied Jacks.
“No problem,” said Woodsey,” we will explain to Rose what you have done for us, there shouldn’t be an issue.”
“Okay,” said Jacks, “lead the way.”

The Ship Inn was in sight and Mayo couldn’t wait to see Mel. He was first to go in.

“Hello everybody.”
Fig was helping Rose and they both dashed around the bar to give Mayo a hug. Mel heard the noise from upstairs and came running down and she threw her arms around Mayo and gave him a big hug and kiss.
“Hey, steady on you two,” said Rose, “Where are the others?”
The doors opened and in came Gaffo, Woodsey, Chrissy and Campbell. Everyone hugged each other.
“How did it go?” Fig asked.
“We rescued Mia she is with Chan at their home getting some rest.”
“That’s great news,” said Mel, “but does this mean you are going home?”
“Not just yet, we are needed for a bit longer," said Mayo.
“That’s great,” said Fig, Mum has kept your rooms so you can stay for as long as you need.”
Just then Jacks and his men walked in. The place fell silent and Rose shouted for Henry.
“It’s okay Rose,” said Gaffo, as he put his arm around Jacks. “He is a changed man. Jacks and his men came with us to rescue Mia, Jacks saved my life and without the good aim of Smudge’s knife throwing skills, we would have lost one of our crew members.”
“Well I don’t know what to say,” said Rose.
Jacks said, “Well let me be the first to say how sorry I am. The way I have treated you for the last

few years I promise that I will behave from now on."

Rose was shocked, she could see a change in Jacks, and she knew it was all down to the influence the boys had on him.

"Let the party commence!" said Chrissy. They all ordered wine and broth and before they had finished their first drink, they were all up dancing and singing. Even the locals were happy to see them again. It was a big surprise to everyone when Jacks got up to dance with them because he wasn't known for smiling and dancing. He was usually miserable, but all the locals could see he had changed and for the better. Henry appeared at the bar and Rose explained everything to him. You could see he was still on edge, but he soon loosened up when he witnessed Jacks actually enjoying himself. Chrissy was up to his old tricks again, talking to the ladies of the night. They were all around him, like bees around a honey pot. Woodsey, Gaffo, Mayo and Campbell were all dancing to the great amusement of the locals. After a long while of dancing Woodsey sat down, one by one they all sat down around the table drinking wine, except for Chrissy, he was busy entertaining the ladies.

Mel and Fig sat down at the table; Fig informed them that Mr Dobbs had sold the five- pound note for two hundred gold coins to one of his associates. Gaffo still had two five- pound notes in his pocket and Woodsey had one in his. Mel had a big

smile on her face. "Maybe we could trade another one with him, because he really didn't want to sell it anyway." "Okay," said Gaffo," we will ask him tomorrow"
Fig would make an appointment with Mr Dobbs. he would be pleased to see them.

"I can't wait," said Campbell, "Helena makes the best cup of tea."
Gaffo stood up yawning, "I'm ready for my pit."
This made everyone yawn, after all it had been a crazy few days at sea, Mel gave Mayo a big kiss, "It's great to have you back."
Mayo replied, "And it's great to be back."
Chrissy came over to them. "Get a room you two."
Mayo replied, "I thought you would be getting your own room tonight."

"No chance, "said Chrissy, "I don't know what I would catch, and you can't get Johnny's anywhere.
Mel asked, "What's a Johnny?"
They all started laughing as Mayo whispered into Mel's ear to explain.

"Eeeeee! exclaimed Mel. "You put it on your willy?"
This just made them laugh even more, while Fig was oblivious.

"I will let you explain it to Fig," said Mayo to Mel.
They all stood up and said goodnight to Jacks, Rose and Henry. There was a nice atmosphere about the place,everyone was in a great mood, so the lads felt more at ease at knowing that there

would be no trouble. It didn't take long, as soon as they hit their pillows, they were all sound asleep. It had been an exhausting few days for them, so they needed all the rest that they could get. Mel and Fig checked in on them. They both had a sad look on their faces, knowing it wouldn't be long before they would leave for good.

"I am so glad you met them," said Mel.

"I think I was meant to and I'm so glad I did," replied Fig. They gently closed the doors over and went to help their mum clear up for the night.

"Everything okay?" said Rose.

"Yes," replied Mel, "they are all sound asleep."

"You both can have the day off tomorrow and spend some time with the boys."

"Thanks Mum," said Fig, "we are going to Mr Dobbs's house, so Mel can come with us.

Mel looked so happy.

"Come on, let's get this place cleaned up and we can all get some rest," said Rose,

"It's been a very busy night tonight. I must say the boys are good for business. Everybody loves them, they even turned Jacks and his crew into half decent blokes."

In the morning Woodsey was the first to wake up. He could hear the noise of horses and carts bouncing along the cobble stoned streets of London. It reminded him of the stories his dad told him of when he was a boy, that's how they used to deliver the fruit and veg to the customers. They were still using horses and carts in the 1950s and not long after, engine driven wagons came on the scene. Gaffo opened his eyes to see Woodsey looking out of the window.

"What are you gorping at."

"Nothing." Just taking in what it's like to live in this century," replied Woodsey.

"I will tell you what it is like," said Gaffo, "you get jumped by ragamuffins, then sail away to fight pirates, then fight Ninjas that are controlled by the Shia, whoever they are; then fight more pirates. Did I leave anything out/?"

"Shut up moaning arse," said Woodsey.

"Are you coming down for food?" Gaffo asked.

"Just give me a minute to get ready." Woodsey walked over to the door, "I will go and see if the other three are up."

"Well hold your nose when you open their door, you know what it smells like first thing in the morning."

"I will," said Woodsey "and that's the best advice you have given me since we got here."

Woodsey knocked on the door, "Come in," Chrissy shouted. Woodsey answered back in a high-pitched cockney accent, trying to sound like a woman, "Is that you Chrissy, you promised you would meet me outside last night, what happened?"

Chrissy replied in a nervous voice, "Errrrm who is it?"

"Who is it?" Woodsey replied, "have you forgotten me already?"

You could hear Chrissy stumbling about trying to get ready. "Hold on a minute, I won't be long." Chrissy opened the door. "Piss off Woodsey, what are you trying to do to me?" Woodsey laughed, which set the rest of them off.

Gaffo heard what Woodsey was doing and laughed to himself while he was getting ready.

"Right, come on," said Woodsey, "let's get something to eat."

They all went downstairs and there was Mel, Fig and Rose with the table set as usual.

"Morning boys," said Rose, "come on now eat up."

"Thanks Rose," said Campbell.

"It's just like being at home here," said Mayo.

As they were all getting stuck into their food, Fig and Mel sat with them.

"Mr Dobbs would like to see all of you today, if that's possible," said Fig.

"That's great," said Campbell, "I can't wait to tell him about the performance of our glass bombs Did he give a time for when he wants us to meet him?"

"Yes, he said about 12 o'clock," Fig replied.

Chrissy said, "That's good, I can go back to bed then."

"No, you can't," said Mel, "we are all going out for the day and you are all coming with us."

"Yes, lazy arse," said Mayo, "all you ever do is slope off to bed."

"Well we have been sailing a ship for days on end," said Chrissy, "so I think I deserve it."

"I don't care," Mel said forcefully. "You are all going out today because me and Fig don't know when you are going to be gone forever."

"All right girl, take it easy," said Chrissy, "I surrender, I will come with you."

"Good, that's settled," said Mel.

Rose came over, "So where are you all going today?"

"We are meeting Mr Dobbs this afternoon," said Fig "and we are going for a look around the town this morning." "That's good," said Rose, "enjoy yourselves and keep out of trouble."

"Don't worry about us," said Woodsey, "our enemies are becoming less these days."

"Unless you're a warlock," said Chrissy.

"I'm not even going to ask," said Rose.

"Come on then," said Fig, "let's go and see the sights."

"Yeah let's walk the misty streets, like a scene from a Dracula movie," said Mayo. Fig looked puzzled, but he and Mel were looking forward to the day. They all headed off and Rose warned them to be careful.

"So where are we going then?" said Mayo.

"There is a street theatre on and it's quite good," said Mel.

"It's not puppets again?" enquired Mayo.

"No," said Mel, "it's real actors."

"That's the way to do it," Chrissy taunted Mayo

about his fear of puppets.

"I'm not scared of puppets," Mayo said.

"Then why did you run from the last one you saw?" said Chrissy.

"Because I didn't expect blood and guts to come out of a puppet's body, did I?"

Campbell was sniffing and scrunching up his face with the smell, "I just can't get used to the smell around here."

"I know," said Gaffo, "you just can't get past it can you. One minute it's sewers and the next spices from the far-off lands."// The roads were very busy with the noise of the horse and carts jostling around each other. There were people in rags and people of wealth. Woodsey was taking it all in, not much has changed the rat race of all times. Mel was excited when they reached the theatre. They went in and sat on the front row. "Oh no!" said Campbell, "it's a Shakespeare play."

"Which one?" said Chrissy. "They are all the same to me," said Campbell.

The play was Midsummer Night's Dream' and, surprisingly, they all enjoyed it and gave a round of applause at the end.

They all set off to Mr Dobbs's house, which was only a fifteen-minute walk. People were nodding and letting on to them, most of them were regulars from the Ship Inn. "It's nice that people are not attacking us anymore," said Mayo. "Don't hold your breath," said Chrissy, "we do have a habit of running into trouble."

"It's okay now though," said Gaffo, "we can just use our special powers."

"What do you mean, special powers?" asked Mel.

"Take no notice," said Woodsey, "he thinks he's Superman."

They arrived at Mr Dobbs house. Fig knocked on the door. The Butler answered, and showed them in. Mr Dobbs was excited and pleased to see everyone. "Come in, how good it is to see you all again, you must have lots to tell me about."

"Where do you want us to start." said Campbell.

"Tell me everything," said Mr Dobbs so they told him the whole story and when they had finished Mr Dobbs was fascinated by it all. "Sounds like you all played your part in the amazing journey and you have come out of it with new strengths."

"Yes," said Woodsey,"

sorry Fig, we did mean to tell you about this, but we thought it might be too much to take in." Fig replied, "You could all handle yourselves before all this anyway, so will this make a difference?" The lads all laughed. "If you think spring heeled Jack could jump high, he's got nothing on us," Woodsey explained.

"We heard you sold the five- pound note Mr Dobbs, said Woodsey.

"I didn't really want to, but the price was too much to refuse. I made a lot of money, so I will give you more."

"It's okay" said Gaffo, "here I have another one

you can keep for yourself."
Mr Dobbs was over the moon, he couldn't believe it, He thought he only had the one five- pound note. He gave Gaffo sixty gold coins. He had received two hundred gold coins for the five- pound note. Fig and Mel were gobsmacked by the amount of money they had received.

"How much is sixty gold coins?" asked Chrissy.

"It would buy you this house and leave you some change," said Mr Dobbs.

"My God, that's life changing," said Mayo.
Gaffo said to Mel and Fig, "Would you like one of these?" They looked at Gaffo who was holding two gold coins, they couldn't believe it, they were going to get a gold coin each. When Gaffo placed the gold coins in their hands, they just stared at them. "Thank you," they both said in unison.
This was the most amount of money they had ever had. "Just be careful with them and spend wisely," said Mr Dobbs..., "so what is the next move?

"Well it depends on what happens when this warlock turns up," said Woodsey, "which is up in the air at the- moment, Chan and Mia are keeping a close eye on it."

"So, you won't be going back just yet?"

"No," said Campbell, "we have all decided to stay and see it through, until Chan and Mia are safe."

"It's very commendable of you all, but you must want to get home," said Mr Dobbs.

"Yes, we do," said Mayo," but they still need our

help, and we will stay until it's over and these gold coins will keep us going for a while."

"How were the glass bombs?" asked Mr Dobbs.

"Brilliant!" said Campbell, "they worked like a dream!"// "I'm glad I could help in some way."

Chan and Mia were at their home. Mia was in a trance. When she came out of the trance, she told Chan, she had seen the warlock, He knows when she is watching him, and he talks to her. He told her he didn't want to harm her and that she shouldn't be worried. He told her that she is more powerful than he is, but he wants to meet her. The Shia had approached him, but this is a personal mission, and he wants to explain when they meet.

Helena walked into the dining room. "Hello everyone! Here are some tea and biscuits for you all."

"Thanks love," said Mr Dobbs.

"Mmmm biscuits," said Campbell, "lovely."

Chrissy shouted, "Quick! Get your biscuits before Campbell eats them all!"

"Shut it you," said Campbell. "Now, now boys there are plenty for everyone," said Helena.

Helena put the tea and biscuits down and left the room.

"Is Helena not staying with us?" said Mel,

"No," said Mr Dobbs, "unfortunately, she has an appointment elsewhere."

"So, you are waiting to see what happens when this warlock shows up?" said Mr Dobbs.

"Yes," said Gaffo, "we are staying just to make sure Mia and Chan are safe..."

"I must say, I was very surprised the way things turned out with Jacks."

"I know," said Campbell, "he saved Gaffo's life, for which he is very grateful, We paid him and his men well for a job well done and they appreciated what we did for them."

Mr Dobbs had a big smile on his face. "Do you realise how much my life has changed since you lot turned up? My inventions have improved immensely, and I just generally feel more inspired."

"Nice to be of service," said Chrissy.

There was a knock on the door. The Butler entered the sitting room, "Sir there is a man called Chan and his daughter asking to meet with you."

"Let them in," said Mr Dobbs.

"As you wish sir." replied the Butler and he went to bring in Chan and Mia.

Mayo said, "It must be important for them to come without setting up a meeting."

Chan and Mia entered the room and greeted everyone. Mr Dobbs offered them tea they both accepted and thanked Mr Dobbs. Chan looked up at them all "you must be wondering why we have come here today."

"Yes," said Woodsey, "normally you would set up a meeting, so it must be important."

"Yes, it is most important, and we knew where to find you."

Did you find us with your telepathy Mia?" asked

Campbell.
Mia smiled, "No we asked at the Ship Inn."
This made them chuckle to themselves.

Mia spoke, "If what the warlock told me is true, there is no reason for you to stay much longer."

"Why is that?" asked Gaffo "and how did the warlock speak to you?// "I had a vision of the warlock and he spoke to me, he told me that he means to bring no harm to me and he wants me to work with him."

"But I thought he worked with the Shia," said Woodsey.

"He does, but he knows my powers are more powerful than his, so he wants to meet and talk about a peaceful solution," explained Mia.

"I thought the Shia wanted you to be their weapon," said Mr Dobbs.

"They do, but the warlock knows they can never make me do the things they want me to do," said Mia.

"I don't get it," said Chrissy, "the warlock does or doesn't work for the Shia and doesn't want to harm you?"

"I know, it's complicated, but we will find out what the situation is when he arrives in two days," said Mia.

"So, two days until we meet the warlock," said Gaffo.

"Yes," replied Chan "and hopefully it will be the end of all this fighting."

"That's something we will have to wait and see

what happens on the day," said Campbell, "but I don't hold much hope."
Mia jumped in quickly, "I am sure the warlock is an honest man."
Suddenly, Mia's eyes started to roll and all you could see were the white of her eyes. She opened her eyes and shouted. "Quick. We need to get to the Ship Inn people are looking for you and causing a scene there."
The lads jumped up straight away and left to see what was happening at the inn. On the way the lads were running and leaping, making them move very quickly and within no time, they reached the inn. The scene at the inn was very upsetting for the lads. The chairs and tables were smashed up and Jacks and his men were lying on the floor with blood pouring from their faces. Behind the bar Henry was on the
floor holding his side, Chrissy bent down to help him, "Are you okay Henry."
"Fine, just a couple of broken ribs, I think."
"What's that on the floor?" said Woodsey.
Henry replied, "It's an ear I bit off one of those bastards that took Rose. I tried to stop them, but there were too many of them. Jacks tried to help, but as you can see, he and his men took a good beating."
"Why would they take Rose?" said Gaffo.
Just then Chan, Mia, Fig and Mel came through the door. "What do you mean?" said Mel, "what's happened to our Mum?"

Fig gave Mel a hug, trying to reassure her that they will bring her back. Mia explained that this was the work of the Shia and the warlock was just a decoy to stop her concentrating on what they were really up to. They took Rose to bargain with Mia because they would not get anything taking Mia again.

Jacks and his men started to come round with a few moans and groans. They all helped the men get to their feet, but they were all hurt, so Mel got the chairs for all seven of them. Mel and Fig fetched some water and cloths. They rinsed the cloths in the water and handed them to the men to clean the blood from their faces. Henry thanked Jacks and his men; they were the only ones that tried to help Rose from being taken. They had all earned respect from him, as they could have been killed. Jacks and his men were happy to help, especially after everyone had been so good to them.

"Did you recognise any of them?" asked Gaffo.

"They are not from around here," said Jacks, "and they didn't look like the ones we fought on the island."

"So, they weren't Ninjas then?" asked Campbell.

"No," said Smudge, "these men were much taller with very tough skin, even our knives just bounced off them."

"What are we dealing with. They can't be human," said Mayo.

"They are human!" said Mia, "but it sounds like they had a spell put on them, like a protective force."

"Yes," said Jacks, "when I tried to punch them it was like hitting a brick wall."

Jacks lifted his hand up to show everyone how much damage he had done to his knuckles, His wrists and hands were swollen, and you could not see his knuckles.

Chrissy asked Mia if she thought the warlock had anything to do with this. Mia didn't think he had; she would have seen him coming. She believed the warlock to be a good man. The Shia had used him to distract Mia. She thought they were using someone else. She had only sensed it because she picked up stressful signals from Rose.

"We can't wait for the warlock to arrive, we must start looking for Rose now," said Woodsey.

"I know," said Mia, "I will try to focus and pick up where she is, but it's not going to be easy."

"They can't be very far though, we got here very quickly," said Campbell.

Henry confirmed they had left only minutes before the lads arrived. Campbell suggested they go to the docks and check the ships.

Mia went into a trance, she started shaking and sweating. Chan looked very worried, he hadn't seen Mia like this before, she was usually very calm. After about five minutes she stopped and started to fall backwards. Chan caught her and sat her down in a chair. Mia had managed to see Rose; she was okay she reassured everyone. She knew she wasn't far away but couldn't see the exact location. Mia had picked up a scent, which was recognisable to her. Woodsey asked Mia if they wanted something from her in return for Rose. They did, but she wasn't prepared to do it. Then she suddenly remembered the scent was whiskey As she blurted it out, without a moment's hesitation the lads, Henry, Jacks and his men all headed to the nearest distillery, which was three miles away on a farm. They thought it best if Mel and Fig stayed at the Inn. They were upset of course but knew they couldn't wish for better people to help find their mum.

Mia told them not to do anything until she broke the spell. Gaffo said to Woodsey, "I'm afraid if Rose is in danger, I'm straight in there."

Woodsey said with a smile on his face, "I know you won't hold back if you see Rose in distress."

Henry led the way as he knew the quickest route. He was running and nobody and nothing was getting in his way, even if there was a brick wall in the way, he would go through it like a rhino. Henry shouted, "Not far now."

Mia could sense magic and knew they were close.

"Here it is," Panted Henry. He pointed to a large wooden barn.

Mia went into a trance. Her eyes rolled showing the whites of her eyes, but this time she didn't shake. Mia was calm, she came around quite quickly. Her first words were, "The warlock is here."

"He can't be," said Chan, "he is days away."

"I am sure I saw him in that barn," said Mia.

"Bloody double-crossing bastard," said Campbell.

"No," said Mia, "it just doesn't feel right. It can't be him-but it looks like him."

"Did you break the spell asked Chrissy.

"I tried, but I'm not sure," replied Mia.

"I wonder if our powers are any good against him," said Chrissy.

Mia replied, "I can't answer that, because I never gave you them, but if you use your mind and do whatever you think is possible, maybe it will work."

Chrissy said. "Yesss, I am going to be the whistler."

"A whistler?" asked Mia.

"Yes," replied Chrissy, "it's the next step to a warlock and he is called a whistler."

"Where did you hear that?" asked Mayo, "and what powers does a whistler have?"

"I saw it on a Hammer House of Horror movie and when a whistler gets upset, he whistles and his victims burn and melt," explained Chrissy.

"But that was just a movie," Woodsey said shaking his head.

"Well, I am going to try it anyway, "said Chrissy.

Henry was getting agitated, "Come on, let's get in there."

As they approached the doors swung open and there stood the warlock. "Welcome and what took you so long?"

"It's not you," said Mia.

"How very observant of you," he said, "yes, you are right, you have been speaking to my weak brother He is warlock Gard, and I am warlock Nada. I am the more powerful one and I am going to have your powers soon." Pointing at Mia.
Henry didn't hold back and ran straight at the warlock, but before he got anywhere near him, he appeared to hit an invisible brick wall and fell backwards to the ground. Dazed, he ran at him again, but to no avail. Some of Jacks men charged towards the warlock, but they all met with the same fate as Henry. Woodsey shouted out to the lads to form a circle and join hands. They started to spin, and a golden light emanated from them. Mia was amazed by what she was seeing, she had no control over them. Nada looked worried, as he had never seen such magic before. He cast a spell on the lads, but it had no effect. Then all of his force ceased, and Henry and Jacks approached to attack They were met by a small army of men, who had lost their sheilding power. Mia knew she didn't need to use her power, as the lads were providing all that was needed. Henry and Jacks were coping well, as the lads were spinning and undoing the spell that the warlock had cast. The lads slowly lowered to the ground.
Nada shouted, "Who are you?"

"We are Scousers," said Chrissy.
Nada raised his two hands, "I demand these boys should be cast back to where they came from."
A faint blue light darted towards them, but noth-

ing happened. Nada looked defeated, but his men kept on fighting. Jacks and his men were doing well, now they were on equal terms. Henry was crushing everyone that came before him. Gaffo was doing roundhouse kicks with his new powers twice as quick with greater strength. All the others were bouncing around, jumping 10ft in the air and punching people out. It was all going well for them, until Henry shouted "Stop!" Everything came to halt and there was Rose with a knife to her throat held by one of the warlock's men. Nada looked smug. "Now I have your attention. All I want is a swop for Mia and her father and the lady can go."

Okay" said Chan, "don't hurt Rose."

"That's more like it," said Nada. "There is no need for all this fuss, just come to me now and the lady can go."

Just as Chan and Mia were about to walk forwards, Chrissy started to do a faint whistle towards the man with the knife. The man suddenly became agitated. He let go of Rose and she ran towards Henry, who grabbed her and carried her back to safety. The man with the knife burst into flames.

"My God," said Mayo, "it really works."

Warlock Nada looked at Chrissy. "You're a whistler."

"Yes," said Chrissy, "and your worst nightmare."

"But I haven't seen a whistler for hundreds of years."

"Well I'm here now and you are finished," said

Chrissy. The warlock was totally defeated.

"Why don't you run back to the Shia and tell them that they are wasting their time for whatever they are trying to achieve and maybe your brother will have something better to tell us." Mia had a smile on her face, "I look forward to meeting your brother, he has more integrity than you will ever have, so just leave and take your slaves with you."

Nada bowed his head in shame and left.

Gaffo looked at Campbell and said, "I didn't see that coming. Who would have thought a story from Hammer House of Horrors would work?"

Mia overheard what Gaffo said, "I think it's what you believe in, that is how your power works."

"But the warlock said that he knew what a whistler was," said Chrissy.

"You are right," said Mia, "there must be some truth in this whistler character."

Henry comforted Rose; she was crying. He hugged and kissed her and promised he would never let anyone take her ever again, with tears in his eyes. Rose looked at Henry and told him that she loved him. They headed back to the Inn, where Fig and Mel anxiously awaited her return. Chan and Mia were pleased that Rose was safe, and nobody was badly- injured, other than a few cuts and bruises. On the way back to the Inn Chan asked Mia what she thought about meeting Gard. She had no problem, as he was more interested in peace than war.

Chan really didn't know what was going to happen next.

Woodsey put his arm around Chrissy, "Well hello, Mr whistler."

Chrissy replied, "I know it actually worked and I almost knew it would before I did it."

"As long as you don't whistle in your sleep," said Mayo.

"Yes," said Campbell, "me and Mayo don't want to wake up in a ball of flames."

Jacks and his men caught up with the lads. Woodsey thanked Jacks and his men for helping them out again. They offered to buy Jacks and his men drinks for the night. They all cheered and were happy at the thought of getting plenty of drinks bought for them.

When they arrived at the Ship Inn it was closed, and people were waiting outside. Rose rushed to the door and banged as hard as she could. The door suddenly opened and there stood Mel and Fig. Rose ran towards them giving them the biggest hug. Henry stood back and watched with a tear in his eye.

Chrissy shouted, "The bar is now open and free drinks for everyone all night!

All the punters cheered as they walked in. Rose called the boys over and thanked them for saving her.

"No need to thank us Rose, it is the least we could do, and it wasn't just us."

"I know," said Rose, "I saw how Jacks and his men

helped with Henry here when they took me and at the barn- they kept me in, thank you all."
Smudge said, "Three cheers for Rose!" and the whole inn erupted with cheers.
Gaffo put a gold coin in Rose's hand to pay for the drinks and told her whatever was left after that night she could keep for herself. Rose kissed Gaffo on the forehead, she was so grateful. As Rose announced the drinks were on the house, the whole inn erupted, and the punters banged their tankards on the bar.

Campbell was sitting there trying to work out how much one gold coin was worth.
Woodsey joined him and tried to explain that if one gold coin could last six weeks and the
average earning in takings a night was three pounds, thirty- eight nights would equate to £114 pounds. In their time if a pub made £300 a night that would equate to £11400. Cambpell yawned as Woodsey explained this mathematical equation to him. He also worked out that they had given Fig, Mel and Rose approximately £1500 each. Woodsey went on to explain that the average wage in this time was £90 a year.
"No wonder Mel, Fig, and Rose's eyes nearly fell out when they were given the coins, said Campbell.

Everyone was getting merry; Jacks and his men were dancing even though they all had battered faces from earlier in the day. Chan and Mia said their goodbyes and headed home. Everyone else carried on drinking and dancing into the early hours and got very drunk.

"I wonder what's next, "said Campbell.

"I don't think the Shia will have any more tricks to play on us," said Woodsey.

"But what is it all about- and why do they need Mia so much when they have their own warlocks?" said Mayo.

Chrissy replied, "I haven't got a clue what's going on."

"I wonder if there is a more powerful enemy that's threatening the Shia?" said Gaffo.

"I don't know," said Woodsey, "if that is the case, why didn't they approach Chan and Mia peacefully and they could have helped each other."

"We are just second guessing here, Let's just wait until we meet this other warlock Gard," said Gaffo.

"It's been quite an adventure up to now hasn't it?" said Mayo.

"It has, but as much as I like the people here, I'm really looking forward to going back home," said Campbell. Chrissy looked at all the lads with a big smile on his face, "I wonder what we will get for the gold coins."

"What do you mean?' we," said Gaffo. The lads looked disappointed as their faces dropped.

"Oh, cheer up, I'm only joking," Gaffo laughed.

"Piss off you," said Chrissy, "I wouldn't put it past you, tight arse." This just made Gaffo laugh even more.

Chan and Mia were at their home, they had only just got back when Mia went into a trance. Chan stood back and let it take place. Mia looked calm, she didn't look distressed, which made Chan feel better. About 30 minutes later Mia came round. She had seen Gard and had a good talk. He didn't know Nada had been there, but he wasn't surprised, as his brother always did the opposite to him and had other ideas of what power meant. She trusted Gard, he was a gentleman and genuine. She thought he was holding back on something. He wanted to explain when they met face to face. Chan was happy with this news, as he was tired of moving and running away from anyone who tried to harm Mia to move back to his beloved China would mean everything to him.

The lads were in full flow, dancing and singing. The locals looked forward to this part of the night.

Woodsey was doing his ska dancing while singing "One Step Beyond."

This got everyone going, even though they weren't sure what to make of it. Gaffo was the first to retire for the night. One by one they all staggered up the stairs. Woodsey, Chrissy and Campbell were the last to go to bed, giggling and laughing while tripping and falling up the stairs. Woodsey crawled to the top of the stairs and turned around to Chrissy and Campbell, put his fingers to his lips "Shhh!,

They all burst out laughing. Just as they were about to enter the bedroom Woodsey said to Chrissy, "No whistling in your sleep."

"Thanks for that," Campbell said looking very worried. Woodsey fell on the bed fully clothed and was asleep in seconds.

Gaffo woke up first in the morning, with the smell of stale beer and wine in the room, he screwed up his face in disgust, but soon realised most of the smells were coming from himself. Woodsey stretched out his arms, gave a big yawn.

"Any need for that?" said Gaffo. Woodsey smiled to himself,

"I feel rough this morning, how about you Gaffo?"

"I feel like errrm, what's the word,Oh yeah, I feel like shit."

Woodsey went to see if Mayo, Chrissy and Campbell were up. He opened the door, "I thought our room was bad,it smells like something has died in here, He waved his hands across his face.

"Open the window and let some air in."

"Are you kidding," said Chrissy, "it smells worse out there than in here."

"Well get ready, we are meeting Chan and Mia later."

"Alright," said Campbell, "give us a minute to get our bearings."

Mayo rolled over and with a groan and said, "Leave me alone and put his hands over his head.

Woodsey went back to his room. "You want to see the state they are in, I thought we were bad, and the room smells like a "tramps" arse."
Gaffo laughed, "I'm glad there are only two of us in this room." Gaffo sat up on his bed. "My God, my head is killing me,Is there anything I can do to get rid of this hangover." Woodsey replied, "A hair of the dog."

"No chance," said Gaffo, "I'm never going to drink again."

"Well just stick your head in a cold bucket of water." Woodsey said laughing.
There was a knock at the door, Chrissy walked in. "Has anyone got anything for a headache?"

"Yes, I've got some paracetamol here," said Gaffo.
"Arrr have you?" said Chrissy.

"No, you knob put your head in that bucket of water."

"Will that help?" said Chrissy.

"No, but it will hide your ugly face for a few seconds."

"Whatever, funny arse," said Chrissy.
Woodsey and Gaffo had a good chuckle to themselves.

Campbell and Mayo shouted from outside the room that they were going to get something to eat they all went downstairs and sat down at the table eating their breakfast when Fig and Mel came to join them.
Mel looked around the place it was a mess, like there had been a battle in there. Fig told the lads

that his mum had hired new staff, with the extra money she had. That meant that Fig and Mel could spend some time with the lads. Mel looked at Mayo and gave him a big smile. "Get a room you two," said Chrissy, what? time are we meeting Chan and Mia?"

"I think it's 10:30," said Woodsey, "they are expecting warlock Gard tomorrow, so I think they just want to go over a few things."

"What do you think about this warlock?" said Campbell.

"Not sure," said Gaffo, "but Mia seems to think he is genuine enough."

"I can't make head nor tail of it," said Mayo, "this Shia lot seem to be going through a lot of trouble to get Mia on their side."

"I know," said Woodsey, "but up to now they are going about it all the wrong way the Shia are facing a losing battle, because Mia is more powerful than anything or anyone they throw at her."

"Even we beat the last warlock," said Gaffo.

"Do you mean I beat the warlock?" said Chrissy.

"Whatever," said Campbell.

Woodsey asked Mel and Fig if they had put their gold coins in a safe place. They reassured him that they had.

It was getting near to 10:00 am, so they made their way to Chan's house. On the way they came across Smudge, who was carrying a bottle of scrumpy. He waved and told them he was on his way to see Jacks, as he wasn't feeling too good.

They all arrived at Chan's house and Chan welcomed them. He and Mia had made a plan, they had decided to meet Gard the warlock aboard his ship. They thought it would be safer than being on land, not only for him but for them also, and also to safeguard against the Shia double crossing them. Mia gave them all a choice whether they would like to go with them and without hesitation the lads agreed to go.Chan had the same ship and crew. If they left at 12 noon they would arrive at midnight. Fig and Mel looked sad again This could be the last time they saw them. This could be the final journey before the spell was lifted and the lads returned home. Mayo went over to Mel and gave her a hug and told her it was a pleasure meeting her, getting to know her. Fig and his mum and Mel started crying, the lads tried to console them all.

Chan and Mia had their stuff ready. The lads agreed to meet them at the docks at 12 noon, meaning they had one hour to get ready to go. They had time to stop at the Ship Inn, to gather a few things and to say goodbye to Rose and Henry. Woodsey put his arms around Mel and Fig reassuring them they would all be okay. He expressed best wishes and if they didn't see them again to live their lives to the full and spend the money wisely. Mel and Fig assured him they would. They said their final goodbyes, with hugs and kisses to

Rose, Henry, Mel and Fig. Rose would miss the lads, they were like a family, even Henry shed a tear. As they made their way from the inn Mayo looked back and could see Mel in floods of tears This made him feel bad, but he knew he couldn't stay. That couldn't happen, as this would bring more upset to his own family back home.

It was getting close to 12 noon. "Come on, we need to get a move on," said Campbell.

"I can see Chan's ship now," said Chrissy, "it looks like it is glowing, like there is a golden cloud around it. There's Chan on the dockside."

Chan was waving to them, to hurry them up.

"Come on, let's not keep him waiting," said Gaffo.

As they boarded the ship Chan led them up the gang plank.

"Quickly," he said, "we must leave straight away."

"What's the hurry?" asked Mayo.

"You will see later, replied Chan."

"What's the golden glow around the ship?" said Gaffo.

Mia said, "Can you see it?"

"We can all see it," said the lads.

"That makes sense," said Chan.

The crew members were all looking around for the glow, they couldn't see it. Mia explained to the lads that it would all make sense later.

The ship headed out of London docks and the crew were hard at work. The lads stood at the starboard side watching old time London drift away. Mia and Chan came over to the lads and Gaffo asked them how far the warlock was from them. Chan told him if they went at full speed it would take two days.

"Two days," said Gaffo, "I thought you said midnight tonight."

"He did," said Mia, "just wait until we get on to the open waters."

"What's with the cryptic clues?" said Chrissy, "where is the warlock anyway?"

"He's on the Mediterranean Sea," said Mia.

"That's miles away," said Gaffo.

"I know," said Woodsey, "and we will probably have some more encounters with more pirates on the way.

"No, it is going to be quite an easy sail this time," said Chan.

"You seem confident about this voyage," said Campbell. Suddenly, the ship began to glow evenmore, even the crew could see it and they were very scared. Then the ship lifted out of the water. The crew were screaming and ran to the cabins. Mayo looked over the side and they must have been 200ft above the water. "Wow" this is fantastic!" he said.

"So, this is your big secret," said Woodsey.

Mia smiled, "Well what do you think?"

"It's amazing!" said Campbell.

All the lads were so happy to be off the water.

"Why didn't we do this when we went to the Isle

of Wight?" Mayo asked.
Mia replied, "I didn't have the power at that time."
"The warlock is going to get a shock," said Gaffo.
"He will," said Mia, "because he is expecting us in two days."
Chrissy was laughing, He couldn't understand why the crew were hiding, at least they didn't have to work. "Lazy gits."
The lads were all in awe with what was happening, there they were, gliding through the air on an old wooden sail ship.
"Who would have thought this would ever have happened to us?" said Woodsey.
Chan said, "I need to say something to you all."
"What is it?" asked Gaffo.
"It's the powers you have. You are going to have them for the rest of your lives, and you choose one power you are best at. Chrissy has chosen to be the whistler, meaning that you all shall choose your own special gift."
"We must be careful," said Woodsey, "because with great power comes great responsibility."
"Those are very- wise words. Which philosopher said this?" asked Chan.
"Spiderman's uncle," said Woodsey. All the lads cracked up laughing.
Chan obviously didn't understand, he was deep in thought muttering to himself, "very wise words, 'with great power comes great responsibility', I must say this to Mia."
"What are you going to be, Woodsey?" said

Gaffo// "I don't know, we can all run fast and leap very high and we are all stronger now than we ever were, so we will have to think carefully and choose wisely."

"I would like to walk through walls, like disappear through them without smashing a hole in them. 'said Chrissy.

"You've had your choice, greedy arse," said Campbell, "but that's a good one I'm having that."

"Go on then Campbell, try it out," said Mayo.

Campbell edged towards the wall and put his face to the timber. His face melted into the timber and he looked around inside the cabin. All the lads were astonished as they watched his head disappear into the side of the ship.

He pulled his head back out and walked over to where the crew were hiding. "Watch this lads" he stuck his head through the

side of the ship. The crew were sitting there looking terrified, all huddled together. He looked over at them and said, "BOO!". The crew screamed, jumped up and ran as fast as they could on to the deck.

The lads were doubled up laughing. Gaffo had a word with the crew and told them not to worry and that no harm would come to them.

"We are not used to this," one of the crew said.

"Neither are we," said Gaffo.

"So, who's next?" said Chrissy. "I wouldn't mind x-ray vision," said Mayo.

"That's because you're a perv," said Woodsey.

"Sod off," replied Mayo.

"Go on then," said Chrissy, "try it."

Mayo stared at the sea. Suddenly his eyes lit up. He described that everything he saw was in 3D. Then he looked over at Chrissy, who said, "Hey you stop looking at my undies!"

"I can see your heart pumping, eeee, it's horrible."

"Just imagine, I can walk through walls and you can see through them," said Campbell.

"Yeah you two will make good bank robbers, or pervs," said Chrissy.

"We can only use these gifts for good deeds you, barmpots," said Woodsey.

"What are you picking Woodsey?" asked Mayo.

"I would like to shape shift into a tiger."

Woodsey concentrated for a while. You could see the anticipation on everyone's face, even the crew. Woodsey

ran across the deck and in mid run he turned into a fully-grown tiger. This freaked everyone out. Then he strolled over to the lads, so they stroked and petted him. He gave out a mighty roar and they all jumped backwards, scared out of their wits. Then he changed back to himself.

"What was that like?" said Gaffo.

"Very strange," replied Woodsey.

Gaffo was next. After thinking deeply for a while, which frustrated the lads, he closed his eyes and outstretched his hands a noise came from the cabin and the door started to shake and vibrate.

The door then flew open and a chair flew out and landed in his hands. Gaffo opened his eyes. “It worked! I can move objects with my mind!”

Mia had seen everything that happened. She believed they had all chosen well. They deserved these gifts, and they suited their characters. Chrissy the whistler, Campbell who can walk through solid mass, Mayo who can see through solid mass, Woodsey who can shape shift into a tiger and Gaffo who can move objects with his mind.

“All these powers will come in very useful for the rest of your time on earth,” Mia told them, “but be careful because people will always try to manipulate you, as I know myself.”

“We would make good spies for the government,” said Mayo.

“No,” said Gaffo, “they would have us wired up in a lab doing tests on us and trying to clone us.”

Mia asked if there was such a thing as cloning. *There was, but only in animals like sheep, for now anyway.*

Two hours later, it was starting to get dark and the view of the stars was mind blowing It was like they were amongst them, as the ship was a couple of hundred feet above the sea. All the lads were stunned by how bright the stars were, they had not seen anything like it before. Mia and Chan joined them on deck. It was a beautiful night. They were not far away from warlock Gard’s ship.

Mia warned the lads to only use their new gifts and powers for good. Gaffo assured Mia that although they would joke about a lot, they were good people. Mia knew this, because the spell had chosen them for their integrity and loyalty, and they had proven this on many occasions. Mia reiterated that they must be careful, as there would always be someone who would try to use them for their powers, for their own means. *Their lives would change, they would be like superheroes. The Scouse Five.*

Mia announced that warlock Gard's ship was in sight. One of the crew members handed a telescope to Mia. She could see there were lots of pirate ships surrounding Gard's ship, approximately one mile away, in a complete circle. The warlock had warned her of this. She thanked the crew member for alerting her and he went back to his post.

Gaffo asked Mia why? are all the pirates, surrounding the warlock. It was the Shia trying to control the situation. Gard and Mia knew they would be unable to do that. Gard was letting them think they had the upper hand. They didn't know that they were above them. It was time to pay them a visit. The ship began to lower down, which made the crew happy although they weren't sure what was about to happen on the water.

As the ship got closer, you could hear people shouting. The crew of warlock Gard's ship looked on in amazement as they landed on the water. Warlock Gard came on to the deck, clapping his hands in excitement. The people, who were part of the Shia, didn't like the warlock's reaction to this unusual appearance from Mia and the rest of the crew.

At last the ship landed in the water to the delight ofthe crew.

"Welcome, welcome," the excited Warlock said, "It's a pleasure to meet all ofyou."

Chan and Mia were the first to board the ship.

"I can't tell you how long I have waited to meet you," said Gard

"Thank you," replied Mia, "it's good to meet you too."

"Come, let's go to my cabin to talk," said Gard.

Mia asked the lads to wait on deck while she and Chan spoke with warlock Gard and to keep a watch for any trouble on the ship.

"This could be it then lads," said Campbell, "we could be on our way home very soon If everything gets sorted with Mia and Chan."

"Don't hold your breath, with everything that has happened to us, I'm saying nothing," Mayo said.

"Don't be such a pessimist," said Gaffo, "let's just hope all goes well."

In the cabin warlock Gard put his hand on Mia's shoulder "You are a very special young lady, and everyone is terrified of you and that is why they want you on their side."

"I don't want to be on anyone's side," Mia replied. Chan spoke up, "My daughter just wants to live a peaceful life and not take sides in all these silly wars."

"I agree, but there will always be someone who will try and control Mia. I have spoken with the Shia and agreed with them, if you go back to China you both can live in peace. They will always watch over Mia, just in case, some other force tries to take her. In a way they will be your guardian," said Gard.

"This sounds like an ideal situation for us both."

"I know, said Gard, "the older Mia gets the more powerful she will become, and they know this."

Outside on deck the lads notice a man with a mask on. Then suddenly he ran to warlock Gard's cabin, opened the door and threw a small object with green mist coming from it. Mayo ran towards the cabin when two men stepped in front of him. They were dressed like the Ninjas they had fought on the Isle of Wight. Mayo used his new speed and agility to leap over these men and turned back to face them. They came at him with flying kicks, but Mayo was far too quick for them. They couldn't believe his speed and tried to land some punches to his face, but this was like slow motion to Mayo. He watched as their fists flew past his head and he slapped their faces without them knowing it was coming. He got bored teasing them, threw a few punches and they both fell to the floor. Mayo used his x-ray vision to look-into the warlock's cabin and he could see Mia, Chan and the warlock on the floor with green mist around them. Then he noticed another figure in the room who was wearing a mask. Mayo tried the door, but it was bolted shut.

He turned to shout to Campbell to go through the wall, but soon realised they had more problems. The pirate ships were pulling up alongside their ship and the lads were preoccupied with handling this situation Chrissy shouted, "Right lads, this should be fun!

"But there are hundreds of them!" said Campbell.

"Watch this!" said Chrissy.

There were twelve ships all together, Chrissy concentrated on them one at a time. He looked at the first one and let out an ear deafening whistle and straight away the sails and the mast caught fire He then turned to the next ship and did the same again. The pirates were all running around trying to put the fires out. This kept them busy and stopped them attacking their ship. However, some did make an attack, and were swiftly dealt with. First a pirate came running towards Gaffo swinging a large sword, he was getting closer. Gaffo closed his eyes, reached out his hand and the sword flew out of the pirate's hand straight to the palm of Gaffo's hand. He lunged at the pirate slashing his cheek with the sword. The pirate fell to his knees holding his face. A few more pirates boarded the ship, but the speed of the lads was just too much for them. The lads were all jumping ten to twenty feet in the air and as they were landing with each jump, they were punching the pirates and they couldn't do anything about it.

Woodsey shouted to Gaffo, "Sod this, I'm fed up with these pricks now!" and in a flash he changed into a tiger.

This changed everything in an instant. All the pirates that were on board jumped overboard. The fear on their faces, as they had never seen anything like this before. Woodsey was still in his tiger form and was prowling up and down the side of the ship and letting out loud roars. You could see no one had any intention of making another attack again. Campbell said, "Okay Woodsey, next time turn into a tiger sooner, so we don't have to mess about with these arseholes."

The fires were still burning on the ships, which was keeping the pirates busy and they looked too frightened to try again. Mayo asked Campbell if he could go through the wall to see if Mia, Chan and warlock Gard were okay.

"But the warlock double crossed us didn't he!"

"No," said Mayo, "they have all been gassed by a green mist and there is someone in there with a mask on."

"I will need a mask."

"We haven't got any."

Mayo walked over to the cabin to have another look.

"Can you see anything." Asked Woodsey.

"Yes, they are all out for the count and that figure

is still standing over them. I can only see an outline of someone" said Mayo.
Gaffo said, "I will try and unlock the door."
He stood in front of the door and placed his hands on it. Within seconds the door started to shake, and they could hear the bolts sliding to unlock. Mayo could see the figure running over to the door to try and stop it opening, but it opened just as the mystery figure got to it and then a green mist came gushing out. It knocked Gaffo back and he dropped to the floor gasping for breath. Campbell and Chrissy dragged Gaffo away and the door slammed shut again. All the lads were coughing and spluttering. They didn't know what it was, and the smell was unrecognisable. Gaffo got to his feet. "We need to check on the crew."
Chrissy checked warlock Gard's ship and Chan's ship. All seemed well.The pirates were still busy pitting out the fires and they were slightly drifting away from them.
Mayo used his x-ray vision to look into warlock Gard's cabin again. They were still on the floor and the figure was still standing over them.

"Mia, Chan and warlock Gard, all have powers," said Woodsey, "but this green gas is keeping them from using any powers at all."

"We will have to watch ourselves," said Campbell, "they know we have powers as well now, so they will want us out of the way, just like Mia, Chan and warlock Gard." Suddenly, Mia's voice came from nowhere, "You are right to be worried."

They all turned to see where the voice was coming from and there was a hologram of Mia standing next to them on the deck of the ship.
Chrissy said, “Are you okay, Mia?”
“Yes, "she answered, “although I’m in a deep sleep, I can still send messages, but I can’t use my powers.”
“What can we do to help? "asked Mayo.
“I’ve seen what you all have done already, but you must be careful you don’t get caught with this sleeping gas, because they will just keep us all contained in a deep sleep for eternity.
The Shia wants us out of the way, so they can rule the world and even though I want nothing to do with them, they will not take the chance of me teaming up with someone else. I would like you all to get on my father’s ship and tell the crew to take you back to London to safety.”
“We can’t do that,” said Gaffo, “there must be another way.”
“No,” Mia said, “you have all done enough for us.In fact, you have all gone beyond what we expected from you.”
Woodsey said, “No, we are not going anywhere until this is sorted out.”
Mayo looked into the cabin. The mystery shadow was leaning over Mia with a knife to her throat. It could see her hologram speaking to the lads. The mystery shadow was trying to stop Mia speaking to the lads.
Mayo shouted out, “That thing is trying to kill

Mia! it's got a knife to her throat!"
Gaffo closed his eyes and put his arms out, Sweat was dripping from his forehead and the knife flew out of its hand and dug into the cabin wall. Mia's hologram started to fade, and her last words were "Thank you."

"What's our next move then? asked Chrissy.

"I don't know," replied Woodsey, "but I was thinking, I wonder if Campbell could walk through the green mist like the solid mass without any effect."

"I will try," said Campbell.

He stood in front of the timber cabin wall and walked into the room Surprisingly the gas didn't have any effect on him. Campbell walked over to Mia, Chan and warlock Gard. He bent down to see if they were okay. He noticed they were still breathing. Suddenly, the figure came running at Campbell with a large knife, but it went straight through him and the figure stumbled across the room. It knew then that it had no chance ofkilling Campbell, so there was no point in trying. Campbell couldn't undo what was happening because if he changed to his normal self the gas would get to him and he couldn't get anyone off the floor because his hands would just pass through them. Campbell went back on deck to talk to the lads. The mystery figure was a woman Campbell relayed to the lads. He could tell by the hand that was holding the knife, it was slim and small.

Gaffo said, "I wonder who this nutty woman is and

what does she want?"
Just then Chrissy started banging on the door shouting, "We know you're a woman, what do you want you lunatic?"
Gaffo shouted through the door, "You will have to come out sooner or later and when that gas runs out, we are coming in there for you!"
They all looked at each other. *Whats? next they were all thinking.*
Woodsey asked Gaffo if he could unlock the door and pull them out with his mind. "I will try, but we will have to stand back away from the gas, or we will all be knocked out by it." They all decided it would be best to get Mia out first because she was the main focus. They all walked to the far end of the ship. Chrissy and Mayo did a quick check around the ship in case they came under attack. All the pirate ships had drifted further away and were smouldering. Gaffo outstretched his hands in front of him. Beads of sweat dripped from his face. He was deep in thought, then the door started to shake.
It was evident this was taking a lot out of Gaffo. Just then the door flew open. Mayo looked with his x-ray vision to see what was happening He could see Mia's body being dragged along the floor, but the woman was holding on to Mia. Mayo whispered to Chrissy about what was happening.
Chrissy said, "That's it! I've had enough of this crazy woman," he let out a high_ pitched whistle.
Mayo watched as the woman's clothes went on

fire, he could see she was starting to panic.

"It's working," Mayo said. No sooner had he said it when the woman came running out with her black clothes in flames. She dived straight overboard into the sea. Mia's body carried on sliding out past the door onto the deck. Gaffo lowered his hands. He looked drained. Woodsey put his arm around him and sat him down.

The gas slowly faded away and Mia started to cough. Campbell ran over to Mia and helped her to her feet.

"Come on, let's get you some water."

"My father," Mia said.

"It's okay, we will get him out as soon as the gas clears from the room," Campbell reassured her.

Gaffo outstretched his hands again, while still sitting down. He moved his right hand in a quick circle motion and an incense steel ball flew out of the room into the sea. Gaffo laughed to himself as he thought, *that is the end of that bloody gas.*

Mia regained her strength and wanted to get her father and warlock Gard out of the room. Gaffo advised her to wait until the gas had completely cleared and they would come around once this had happened. Mia couldn't wait, so she conjured up a spell and waved her hands in the direction of the cabin. Suddenly, a strong gust of wind came from nowhere, swirled into the cabin and cleared what was left of the gas instantly.

Mia and the lads rushed into the cabin and as they entered the room Chan and Gard were already sitting up, recovering from the effects of the gas. They both got to their feet and walked outside. Mia needed questions answered. She wanted to know what was going on. Gard didn't see it coming, someone must have had cast a spell over the ship.

Chrissy shouted, "Woman overboard! They all looked over the side of the ship and there was the woman who had caused all the trouble. Mia looked surprised and everyone could see Mia knew this woman. Gaffo asked Chan if he knew this woman.

Chan nodded his head, "Yes" In a shocked whispering voice,

"It's my niece."

"Your niece? Why would your niece, want to harm you?

"That's what we are about to find out."

They lowered a rope down to her and pulled her up to the deck. Mia bent down to her cousin and looked at her straight in the eyes.

"What's going on-why would you do this?"

She couldn't respond and was shivering from the cold sea water. Warlock Gard stepped in, "I don't think she meant any harm to us; you can see the poor girl is terrified."

"What's your name?" asked Gard.

The girl responded in a shaky shivering voice,

"My name is...," but before she said anything, Mia answered for her.

"Her name is Nicki and we are cousin's." "
" Okay Nicki," said Gard, "tell us why you gassed us and how you got here without me noticing you."
Nicki looked sad. She took a deep breath and explained why she acted the way she did. The Shia came to her village and threatened her family. They said if she didn't help them, they would kill her mother. Gard was confused because the Shia had come to him to make a peaceful outcome of all this. Nicki explained to him that was just a distraction. They have another warlock who cast a spell so he wouldn't be able to detect the pirate ships and that is how she got there.
Gard said, "So my brother is still helping the Shia."
Mia put her arms around Nicki and promised her she would make everything better and that their family would be okay.

Mia asked the lads for one last favour.
"What is it?" asked Woodsey.
"I would like you all to come to China with us."
The lads all agreed that they would go to China. She promised them once the mission was complete, she would send them all back home.
Chrissy said, "I've never been to China and I haven't got a passport."
The lads all burst out laughing, but Mia didn't get the joke.
Mia shouted, "Okay everyone, let's all board our ship."
They all followed her onto the ship. All the crew

were okay, but they knew what was coming next. As soon as everyone was on board, the ship lifted out of the water again and shot off into the sky. Nicki couldn't believe her eyes, she was amazed.

"My God," said Campbell,"what speed are we doing?"

Mia answered, "We are going very -fast, so-fast we will be in China in six hours,"

"That's faster than Concord," said Mayo, "how come we can't feel any wind?"

Mia just smiled and walked off to talk to Nicki and Chan.

Mia reassured Nicki not to worry about her mother and family. She promised her that nothing will happen to them. Nicki smiled and thanked Mia. Chan told Nicki to go to their cabin and get some rest. She thanked him and went to the cabin to get dry and some much-needed sleep.

As soon as Nicki was out of ear shot, Chan asked Mia, how could she make a promise like that, when they didn't know what to expect. Mia told her father that her powers were at their highest peak, giving her a great advantage over the enemies. Since Chan had made the spell to bring the boys to help them, she has felt it growing every day and was at the point where nothing was impossible to achieve. She had put protection around her family and friends so the Shia can't use them against her, but she didn't know if the spell would carry on when the boys had left. That's why she wanted them to come to China, to make sure the Shia could see what she was capable of achieving. She may still have the power when the boys have gone but didn't want to take the chance until the mission was complete. Then they could live without fear once and for all. Chan quizzed Mia further on what she was capable of doing. He was shocked to hear that she could freeze oceans, blank out the sun or even set fire to forests. It made sense to Chan now why the Shia tried to put her in a state of sleep, so that she couldn't use her powers against them. He wondered how she would help Nicki's mother and the rest of the family. Suddenly, Mia went into a trance and an image of Chan's sister, Su Lee, who was in Nantong, China, appeared for Chan to see. She was inside the house; Chan shouted her name. Mia encouraged Chan to speak to her, she could hear him. During this time the lads were on deck and they could hear Chan talking to an image next to Mia. They came in to see what was going on. Chan was getting emotional, as he hadn't seen Su Lee for many years. Su Lee was also crying when she heard Chan's voice. She asked if Nicki was okay and was glad to hear she was safe. This made her happy.

Mia told Su Lee not to be frightened, as no one could hurt her or any of her family ever again. Su Lee wasn't sure about this as they were watching the house and would follow her when she left. Mia promised Su Lee that they would never follow her again. Then Mia waved her hands, and a strange wind blew around Su Lee's house. Two men from the Shia were standing outside the house and looked confused. When the gust of wind stopped one of the men went to walk towards the front of the house, he was lifted up in the air and thrown backwards 30ft. Then the two men ran away fearing for their lives this would happen to anyone who would threaten her or follow her or any member of their family. Su Lee said she would let their family and friends know they need not fear anyone anymore. Su Lee thanked Mia and the image of her faded, but before they lost contact, Chan shouted to Su Lee that they would see her very soon. Su Lee was so happy to hear this news.

Chrissy was first to comment, "That was better than an action movie."

Campbell replied, "This whole Thing has been like an action movie from the moment we arrived here."

"Don't worry," said Chan, "once we get to China and get things resolved, you all will be going home soon after."

Chan looked happier than he had done for a long time. He turned to Mia and suggested they get some rest and to let Nicki know that her mother was safe.

Mia and Chan went to their cabin. Woodsey looked puzzled and Gaffo asked him what was up. Woodsey shrugged his shoulders and said, "I don't understand why we need to go to China when Mia is more than capable of looking after her family now."

“She must have her reasons I don’t think she would drag us all to China for no reason.”

“I suppose you're right.”

Chrissy started jumping in the air.

“What are you doing?” Asked Campbell.

“I’m bored "he said" it feels strange while the ship is up in the air.”

“Well you won’t go over the side,” said Gaffo.

“Why not?” said Chrissy.

“Think about it, we are travelling faster than Concord and we can’t feel the wind, so that means we must have a force around us.”

“Wow! I never even thought of that!” said Mayo. So, they all started jumping in the air 10-20 ft at a time, while grabbing hold of the mast and looking across into the sky.

“I hope we can still leap this high when we get back home," said Campbell.

“I know we will be able to leap into trees and hide from everyone,” said Woodsey.

This made Gaffo laugh.

“What are you laughing at?” Asked Woodsey.

“Why would you need to hide from anyone when you can turn into a tiger?”

Woodsey laughed, “I get what you mean.”

After about an hour of the lads leaping around Mayo had had enough and went to get some sleep. The lads all decided to do the same.

Warlock Gard was in his cabin reflecting on everything he had just witnessed. He realised that Mia could be dangerous if she lost her temper

while using her powers. With this thought in his mind as he lay on his bed and closed his eyes.
All the lads were fast asleep when suddenly they could hear people talking and the sound of water. They all jumped off their beds to see what was happening. When they looked outside all the crew were looking over the side of the ship. They must have landed because the crew only ever looked over the side of the ship when they were on water. Mia, Chan, Nicki and warlock Gard were at the front of the ship. The lads went to join them.

"Morning," said Gaffo.

They all turned around, nodded and wished them all a good morning.

"Where are we exactly?" asked Campbell.

"We are on the Yangtze river by Nantong," replied Mia, "it's where my family are from and it's where we are finally going to put things right for good."

"That's more like it, more fighting to be done," said Chrissy.

"Hopefully not," said Chan, "but if need be, we will have to."

Mia looked at them all very seriously and told them she wanted them to stay close. To get this done smoothly without anyone getting hurt. So, she ordered them ashore. She wanted to visit Su Lee first, to see if her spell was still working and keeping everyone safe.
They reached the bank of the Yangtze river, where there was a small crowd of people waiting to greet

them with huge excitement. They must have seen them coming out of the sky. They shook everyone's hands with great enthusiasm. "These are a happy lot, aren't they?" said Campbell.

"I know," said Mayo, "they are almost shaking my brains out."

All the lads found this amusing. Chrissy was saying, "How do you do. How do you do," to everyone he shook hands with. This made everyone laugh. Mia said, "Come now we must move on." The lads could see that the locals recognised Nicki, Mia and Chan, but were unsure of Gard, maybe it was his pointed hat.

"How far is your village?" asked Gaffo.

"It's a couple of miles away," replied Chan.

"A fifteen-minute walk then," said Woodsey as he rubbed his hands together in excitement.

As they walked along the road lots of people were nodding and letting on to Nicki, Mia and Chan, but they gave the lads strange looks.

"Why are the staring at us?" asked Campbell.

"They haven't seen many Western people before," said Chan, "it's all new to them."

"They seem cheerful enough people," said Mayo// "Yes, they are," said Mia, "but we have to deal with the not so cheerful people as well."

"Bring it on," said Chrissy. This brought a smile to Mia's face.

All the village houses were made of bamboo and looked very weak and flimsy.

"They could do with a good bricklayer here,"

said Chrissy, "the three pigs wouldn't stand a chance in these houses." "You're not wrong there Chrissy," said Woodsey, "I think that makes the Shia the big bad wolf."

As they got closer to Su Lee's house, all the neighbours were smiling. It looked like they had been under the rule of the Shia and they knew things were about to change. Su Lee came running out of her house shouting Nicki's name and threw her arms around her, hugging and crying. Both were in tears. They were both happy to see each other. Su Lee thanked and kissed Chan and Mia. They went inside the house to talk.

Before entering the house, Woodsey took off his shoes.

"What are you doing?" said Campbell.

"It's a tradition to take your shoes off before entering a house." And just as he said it, Mia, Chan and Nicki took their shoes off.

"I told you," said Woodsey.

"Okay, smart arse," said Campbell.

Su Lee offered everyone tea. "Oh yes, please," said Mayo.

"It won't be a Tetley teabag you know," said Woodsey, "but I'm sure it will be nice."

They all sat down on mats on the floor and Su Lee gave them small cups and poured the tea. They all took small sips and were surprised how nice it tasted. They expressed their appreciation to Su Lee. Mia introduced them all. Su Lee commented on how strange the names were except for Mayo,

she knew a lot of Mayo's. This made the lads laugh. They teased Mayo and told him he would fit in around there.
Mia asked Su Lee how she was. She felt much better now that they were there and had not seen the Shia since Mia had appeared to her. She had felt safe since then. *That was the way it was going to stay.* Warlock Gard wanted to know if the Shia were controlling many people around there. They had been until the wind came and Mia appeared to her, the whole place felt better. Mia was intrigued by this. Her spell had gone more widespread than she intended it to, but this made her happy and warlock Gard could see this on Mia's expression.

They were all wondering what would happen next, when Mia told them that they would sit and wait. The Shia knew that they had arrived, but they couldn't come near them, the spell won't let them. They can come if their intentions are good and they don't threaten anyone, but if they do show any signs of bad, then the spell will come into effect. Mayo asked if warlock Nala could break the spell. He couldn't break the spell because it was above and beyond him to do this. Mia contemplated lifting the spell to encourage the Shia to approach them, so they could talk. Chan reminded her that the villagers were all happy and this would bring unrest to them if the Shia came back there. He did suggest going outside the village to discuss terms with the Shia. Warlock Gard agreed this was a good idea. The lads and Gard would be there to protect them, so they made a plan to set off the next day.

"Is it going to be safe for you Mia?" asked Gaffo.

"Yes. They can't harm me now, but they will always try and harm people I love and care for."

Woodsey asked Mia to lift the spell on them when they met with the Shia, because they wanted to show them their strengths and that they can protect themselves, so they would keep away from their friends in London. Mia agreed to lift the spell when the Shia came. Warlock Gard also wanted Mia to lift the spell on him. He wanted to speak to his brother through mind control and wouldn't be able to do that with a spell cast upon him. Mia promised she would do this.

There were a few Shia just outside the village and every time they took a step towards it, a strange feeling would come over them. They were dressed in black like the Ninjas were at the Isle of Wight and little did they know that they could just walk into the village if they meant no harm to anyone. Further away from the village there were many more of the Shia and warlock Nala was with them. One of the main leaders of the Shia was there and his name was Kim. It was up to him to try and overpower Mia once and for all. He approached warlock Nala and asked him if he could lift the spell on Mia and the village. Nala had already tried and failed to lift the spell. It was a spell he had never encountered

before. Nala was no use to him, or the Shia and

Kim thought about having him killed. He ordered two ninjas over who were holding long swords and contemplated cutting off Nala's head and sending it to his brother. He had second thoughts, as he tapped his finger on his mouth. He ordered the two Ninjas to watch over him and kill him if he tried to escape.

Nala felt betrayed, but he knew no one could stop him from leaving and one thing you don't do is upset a powerful Warlock. He could also read Kim's mind, whose aim was to threaten his life to get to his brother, but Nala still loved his brother deep down and this made him furious. Nala only sided with the Shia to get to Mia and find out more about her powers. He never intended to harm her in anyway. Nala suddenly raised his hands and put the Ninjas into a deep sleep. He walked towards the village. Kim shouted, "Stop him!"

But no one tried. They all knew it would be futile to try. All the villagers were very wary of Nala as he nodded and smiled to them. Gard could see Nala approaching. Mia could see him too, but she knew he meant no harm to them. Nala walked straight up to Gard and said, "Hello brother." Gard had a smile on his face as they hugged each other. Chrissy said, "So we have another warlock on our side." "Looks that way, said Gaffo, "they might as well give up now."

Gard introduced Nala to Mia. "It's a pleasure to meet you at last," said Nala.

Mia nodded her head and smiled, “It’s okay, I know you have been a threat to me and now we can get to know each other peacefully.”
Nala smiled. This is what he wanted, a peaceful resolution. Gard then introduced Nala to Chan and the lads. He knew all about the lads, he had been watching them since they arrived and knew how loyal they were and how they had helped Chan and Mia and also about the powers they possessed// Gaffo said, “You’ve been busy watching us, Then.”
Nala just smiled and winked at Gaffo.
Nala, Gard, Mia and Chan walked off to discuss what would be best for their next move. Nala explained, “I am not actually in my full body form but only in a trance as it would be a miracle for me to arrive here so quickly.to think them fools were going to try and kill me and he gave out a load laugh.

Chrissy said, “Did you see him wink at Gaffo? I think he fancies him.”
They all burst out laughing, except Gaffo, he told them all to piss off.

Mia came over to the lads to inform them of the plan. They would go outside the village and Mia would lift the spell so the Shia could engage with them. She was hoping for a peaceful outcome, but Nala had told her that Kim wanted her dead and anyone that is with her, the lads told her not to worry, they were right behind her, whatever happened. Mia was so grateful to the lads; they had done so much for her and her family. The plan was they would engage with them and if they showed any sign of force they would have to fight them Let them think they have a chance, then show them what they are dealing with, using all their powers. The lads were agreeable to the plan.

Mia led the way as they headed out of the village with Chan, Nala, Gard and the lads by her side. They drew close to Kim and his army. There were hundreds of them. The lads moved to the front. Kim stepped forward with many men alongside him. "Is this all you have? "why don't you come with us now Mia and no-one will get hurt?"

"That's not going to happen," said Woodsey.

Kim was furious and ordered his men to attack. The lads sprang into action straight away all jumping in unison 15 ft into the air and landing on the first five Ninjas. Then, with great speed, running back and forth to Mia then to the front line, punching more Ninjas out. Kim ordered his men back. He shouted, "Take Aim!"

Then a hundred archers fired their bows with fire burning at the end of the arrows. As the arrows descended towards them Gaffo put his arms up straight then pointed to the left then to the right. The arrows suddenly changed direction and landed to the left and right of them without anyone being harmed. Chrissy could see the archers loading up again and Gaffo looked drained, so he gave out a loud whistle. The archer's bows caught fire and they dropped them to the floor. Kim was astounded. Thirty Ninjas came running towards them Woodsey ran straight at them and changed into a tiger. The Ninjas came to a sudden halt as Woodsey prowled side to side roaring at them.

Mia could see the lads were getting tired, so she walked forward and asked them to step back. She waved her hand in the air and the whole army including Kim were lifted 10ft into mid-air. They were helpless. Mia spoke, "Let it be known today that I fear no one especially the Shia and anyone associated with them. I could kill you all with a click of my fingers," As she held her fingers together, Kim looked nervous.

"But I won't do that. I'm going to put you all back on the ground now. Please don't try to bother me, my family or my friends, ever again, or there will be consequences for your actions."

With that all the men came back to the ground and most of them didn't hang about for long and soon they had all fled, except for Kim. He was paralysed and could not move. He looked nervous as Mia and Chan approached him. Mia stood inches away from his face saying, "Don't worry, I'm not going to harm you."

Beads of sweat ran down his face.

"You are just my messenger to the leaders of the Chinese Empire. That's right, I know that the so-called Shia are run by them and I have known for some time, so I want you to take a message to your leaders, That I can see everything. I can turn night into day and day into night, Turn the tides. Mia closed her eyes and darkness descended in an instant changing daytime into night- time. You could hear gasps coming from the villagers. Even Chan, the lads, Nala and Gard were amazed. Mia opened her eyes and light ascended changing back to daytime. Mia looked straight into Kim's eyes saying, "This is nothing, I can paralyse a whole army from hundreds of miles away if I wish to, especially if I sense harm from them, Go back to your leaders and tell them what you have witnessed today and let them know I will be watching and listening to everything they do and say." Kim could suddenly feel movement back in his legs. He turned and walked away slowly, but he didn't feel any threat from Mia at this time, as he had no intention of causing her anymore harm.

Mia and Chan walked back towards the village, the lads, Nala and Gard walked with her. Chrissy put his hand on Mia's shoulder and said, "Well I don't think anyone will mess with you anymore. I am just glad we are good friends."
Mia giggled, "You have all been so good to me and my father, I honestly couldn't have done it without you."
"Not a problem," Replied Campbell, "I think it's time to celebrate."
All the villagers ran towards them. Nala whispered into Gard's ear, "I'm glad I chose to come on

your side."
Mia was about 20ft away from Nala and shouted, "I heard that!
Nala and Gard found this very amusing and smiled at each other.

As they entered the village the atmosphere was great. Everyone was happy, hugging and kissing each other. They were all bowing and kissing Mia's hand; she was like the new Queen. Mia was happy for these hardworking people, who had been treated so badly in the past.

Mia finally arrived at her house and stood at the front door with Chan, Gard and Nala. Mia was looking for the lads, but they were surrounded by all the locals. They were feeling their clothes because they had never seen clothing like it. Mayo said, "if you think these clothes are good, you should see my Lacoste trackie."
The people just smiled at him, even though they couldn't understand a word he was saying. Campbell spotted Mia waving them over to the house.
"Look. I think Mia wants us to go over to the house. We better do as she says, said Woodsey, "we don't want to upset her."
They all laughed and walked towards the house, which took some time as they shook hands with everyone on the way.

They all went inside the house and sat in a circle with their feet tucked under them. Mia spoke first, "I think it's time that you all go back home to your families."

"Are you sure?" said Gaffo.

"Yes," replied Mia, "you have all been so helpful to me and my father and it's time for you all to return home."

"Maybe we should stay for one more day," said Woodsey,

"just in case anything happens."

Mia just said, "No, you have all kept your word and stayed to help me and now it's my turn to help you."

"But what if they come back?" said Mayo.

"Don't worry, they won't, and Gard and Nala are staying here with us now as my watchful, trusting friends."

"Can we just stay tonight then?" Asked Chrissy, "we wouldn't want to miss out on the celebrations."

"Okay, okay," said Mia, "you may stay tonight, but tomorrow you must all go back home." The lads all looked at each other nodded their heads and smiled.

The celebrations started in the village later that evening. There were fireworks lighting up the sky.

"Yes!" said Chrissy, "it's bommy night!"

"No, it's not," said Woodsey, "the Chinese always have fireworks to celebrate any occasion, it's a tradition. The best ones are the firecrackers, they chase you across the floor. Look There's one!" Woodsey pointed to a firecracker.

"Wow, that's brill!" said Campbell, "I need to get myselfone ofthose."
Mayo went over to the man who had a bunch of firecrackers in his hand. Mayo pointed at them. "Can I have one ofthose, please?"
The man didn't understand what he was saying but gave him one anyway and smiled. Mayo gave him thumbs up to thank him.
"Here you go, Campbell."
There were candles everywhere, so Campbell picked one up and lit the firecracker. The firecracker started banging instantly, Campbell nearly shit himself, let go of it and it dropped to the floor. It snapped and banged around his feet and followed him as he tried to run away from it. All the lads were crying with laughter. It finally burnt out. Woodsey was still laughing, "You're supposed-*haha!* You're supposed to throw it away from you."
"Now you tell me. Thanks for that," Campbell sounded very annoyed.

Kim had arrived back to meet the elders of the Shia, which was basically the leaders of the Chinese Empire, as well as other countries leaders. Kim could see the anticipation on the elders' faces, but the news he had wasn't what they wanted to hear. Kim explained that no one could manipulate Mia in any way, shape or form. One of the elders raised his hand. Kim stopped talking. "What you are saying is that this little girl can do

as she likes, and we can't do anything about it."
Kim replied, "She has no wish to have any confrontation with us, as long as we don't threaten her or her family and friends. Mainly her village."
"So, you are telling us to just leave her alone and she will not intrude in our dealings," said the elder.

"Yes, that's basically it," said Kim.

"What kind of power does she have?" said the elder.

"Well if you show any ill will towards her or anyone she knows; she will demonstrate her powers. I have witnessed her turn night into day. She raised my whole army off the ground and paralysed me so I could not move any part of my body," said Kim.

"So, she could have killed you all," said the elder.

"Yes, she could have," said Kim.

"What about Nala?" asked the elder.

"Nala doesn't have the powers that Mia possesses," said Kim, "plus Nala has joined forces with Mia and his brother Gard."
The elder asked Kim if he knew why Nala had joined forces with them. Kim told the story of how he tried to use Nala against Gard and had even threatened to kill him, if he betrayed him, but Nala had an alliance with his brother and Kim couldn't contain him any longer. As Nala was determined to win back trust from his brother. The Elder asked what he knew about the five young foreign men that Mia had by her side. Kim told

him of their great powers,that they could jump to any height and move at great speed. One had the power to make fire by a high-pitched whistle. One can move objects with his mind and one can shape shift into a tiger. The other two have powers, but he had not seen them being used.
The elder thought it interesting why Mia would need these five young men if she possessed such great powers herself. Kim couldn't answer this question, as he had no idea why. Kim also explained that they couldn't launch an attack on her, as she sensed hostilities from afar. The elder that was doing all the talking was seated in the middle and had two elders either side of him. He had a discussion with them. Kim could hear them whispering to each other. The middle Elder expressed intention to attack her, *with their greatest weaponry and end this once and for all.* Suddenly, the room started shaking, He looked at the elders. Their mouths were moving, but no sound came out. The room stopped shaking; the elders looked scared. Kim could hear them again, but the middle elder was shaking and his voice trembling. He pointed at Kim, "Why didn't that affect you?" Kim answered, "Because I don't wish Mia harm anymore. I have witnessed her great powers and it would be futile to try to harm her or try to kill her. If you wish to carry on trying, her wrath will grow stronger. I will take no further part in it." Kim turned and walked out of the room. The elders dared not oppose him in case Mia was protecting

him and they were right to think that as Mia was watching and listening everything that was said.

CHAPTER EIGHT

Back at the village Mia was in her room alone. She was in a trance, Gradually she awoke from the trance and felt good that the Shia were finally convinced of what she was capable of achieving.That her powers were so great, they couldn't win no matter what they tried against her. Now she could live her life in peace.

The celebrations were in full flow in the village and the lads had been offered tea most of the night.

"I'm fed up," said Chrissy, "all they drink is tea, I know it's the tradition, but I need a beer."

Gaffo spotted Chan and shouted over to him. "Is there anything stronger than tea that we could sample?"

Chan said, "Follow me." Chan led them to an old friend of his called Mr Woo. Woo blended the finest whiskey in China.

A very tall thin man approached them from the house. He had a very long wispy white beard.

"Is he a wizard?" asked Campbell.

"No," said Chan, "but he makes a mean potion."

Mr Woo gave Chan a hug. They had a conversation

in Chinese. Mr Woo went back in the house and came out with seven small cups. He handed them all a cup and they all knocked the drink back in one go.

"Oh yes, that's a fine drop," said Chrissy.

"Fire water," said Mayo in a croaky voice.

"You like?" said Mr Woo in broken English.

"Yes, very nice Mr Woo," said Woodsey.

Chan left them in the capable hands of Mr Woo, as he wanted to check on Mia. The lads were happy to carry on drinking the whiskey. Chan arrived back at the house and knocked on Mia's door. "Are you okay, Mia?"

"Yes, come in Father."

Chan entered the room and noticed Mia looked drained.

"What's happened?" said Chan looking very worried.

"It's okay," said Mia, "I have seen the elders of the Shia and i have given them a warning. I think they have got the message." "That's good news," said Chan.

The party was in full swing. Chan and Mia returned to the celebrations. Chan squeezed Mia's hand. *This is wonderful. He thought he would never see the day, when peace would finally come to the village again, but it was here at last.* Mia looked at her father. "It is finally over. The Shia have seen what I can do, so we will not get any more trouble from them."

Chan wondered if Mia would still have the same

powers when the boys returned home. Mia didn't know, her powers had dramatically changed since they arrived. She would just have to wait and see and hopefully she would.

Mr Woo was smiling and clapping every time the lads knocked back a shot of whiskey. He thought it was highly amusing because he knew how potent it was. The bottle was soon empty. Chrissy shouted. "Any more please Mr Woo." Pointing to the empty bottle."
Mr Woo nodded his head and went inside to grab another bottle. Moments later Mr Woo came back out giggling to himself and handed the bottle to Chrissy. Chrissy smiled at Mr Woo and said, "What's so funny?"
Mr Woo walked Back into the house still laughing to himself. Woodsey said, "He thinks it's funny that we are drinking so much of his rocket fuel. We will probably not wake up tomorrow."
"That means one more hangover and one more day here," said Campbell.
"No way," said Mayo, "as much as I like being here and helping out, I think it would be good to finally get home and get back to normal."
"What's normal?" said Gaffo, "it's never going to be the same again, especially with our superpowers and what we are capable of doing."
"I know, said Mayo, "what are we going to use the gifts we have got for exactly? I suppose we will just see how it all pans out when we get back.

You never know, we might lose them when we get back to our own time and surroundings."

"I hope not, said Chrissy, "I quite like being a whistler."

"I agree with Chrissy," said Gaffo, "I wouldn't mind still having the ability to move things with my mind."

"I think we all wouldn't mind having these abilities when we get back," said Woodsey, "now let's finish the bottle and get some sleep."

The lads finished the bottle and thanked Mr Woo. As they walked away Mr Woo was waving and continually saying Bye, bye, bye!" Woodsey smiled at Mr Woo,then turned to the lads. "He's as mad as a box of frogs."

The celebrations were still in full swing with people dancing and setting off fireworks. The villagers looked so happy with their newfound freedom and not having to live in fear anymore. Campbell spotted Mia, Chan and Su Lee sitting with a group of people. "Come on lads, let's say goodnight to Mia and her family."

They all stumbled over. "Hello everybody," slurred Chrissy.

Mia shook her head, "I think you all should sit down here."

"No, it's okay, Mia," said Gaffo, "we are going to bed now."

"No, sit down," Ordered Mia. The lads looked at each other.

"I think we better sit down," said Gaffo.

"Here," said Mia, "drink this tea." And she gave them all a small cup of tea.

"It's okay Mia," said Chrissy, "I don't like tea."

"Drink it," Mia said loudly.

"Ooow, she told you", said Mayo.

"All of you," Mia reiterated.

They immediately drank the tea, without hesitation and within seconds they were all sober.

"Wow!" said Gaffo, "I feel as fresh as a daisy!

Chrissy's reaction was, "What a waste of whiskey that was. This made Mia laugh. Mia stood up. "Seriously, I need you all to be focused on your return home tomorrow, and that means having a clear mind and body for your movements in time travel. Also you all need to watch out in the future that you don't get intoxicated and show off your abilities in front of people who may take advantage of you."

"Like who? said Chrissy.

"Criminals for one," said Mia, "and also heads of state or

leaders of armies, as you have seen what's happened to

me since you came here."

"We understand," said Woodsey. "We will be careful."

Mia bowed her head and bid everyone good night. The lads stood up and followed her to the house for a good night's rest, to get themselves ready for what lay ahead. They all shared the same room that night, but none of the usual antics were

played out.
Campbell said, "I've never felt so good. I feel totally refreshed,"
"so, do I," said Mayo, "do you think we could get the recipe to cure hangovers, "We will make a fortune out of that!"
"Good idea," said Woodsey, "we'll ask Mia for the potion ingredients tomorrow."
This made them all laugh as they nodded off.

The next morning everyone woke up early and feeling good.
"I wonder what's for breakfast," said Woodsey.
"Probably rice with something or other," said Chrissy.
"I don't mind," said Mayo, "I love Chinese food."
"Same here," said Campbell.
There was a knock on the door.
"Are you all awake?" it was Su Lee.
"Yes, come in," said Gaffo, "we are all decent.
Su Lee entered the room, "We have food for you to get ready for this special day."
They all went into the next room where they sat cross-legged with bare feet.
"I hope you have washed your feet Chrissy," Mayo whispered in his ear, giggling.

Mia, Chan and Su Lee joined them for breakfast. Bowls were brought in and to their surprise there were slices of bacon, which they could not believe, and bread as well.
"Wow, this tastes lovely!" said Gaffo.
Mia smiled, "I thought you would enjoy this, so I

asked the local farmer to get me some pig meat for your last meal here."

"Yum, yum," said Chrissy with his mouth full, putting a thumbs up to Mia.

Mia was happy that they enjoyed the food so much and not a scrap of meat was left. When they had all finished, Mia told them that she had no feeling of harm towards her or the village from the Shia, so it

was all looking good and that we should get prepared for our journey home.

"Are we going back on the floating ship first?" asked Mayo.

"No," replied Mia, "I'm hoping to transport you all back to where you came from when I first cast the spell."

"That's a pity," said Mayo, "we won't be able to say goodbye to Fig, Rose, Mel, Big Henry and all the rest of them in London."

"I'm sorry," said Mia, "but this will be the easiest way for me to achieve your safe return home."

"Okay, that's fine," said Woodsey, "we understand."

Mia asked the lads to go and lay down again on the beds and try and clear their minds. She would come in later to talk to them all. Over the next hour the lads slipped into a deep sleep. Mia knew this would be the last time she would see the five lads from Liverpool because she knew they wouldn't wake up from their sleep in this place. She didn't want to tell them this before

they lay down, that they would be travelling forward through time. Mia sat in the middle of the lads as she cast her spell. The room began to shake, but not the rest of the house. Mia held her hands up in the air and chanted, "Return, return, return the five to the place where they arrived."
The lads started spinning as they linked hands in a circle. They were still laying down next to Mia and slowly vanished from sight. The lads continued to spin, but now fully awake. It was the same sensation as the first time it happened. This seemed to be lasting a long time, but it was only a few minutes, then gradually it slowed down.

It was misty. There were people around them as they tried to get their breath. As the mist cleared there stood Fig, Rose, Mel, Big Henry, Jacks, Smudge, Mr Dobbs, Helena, friends of Jacks and the locals from the inn.

"Wow, we are back in London! said Gaffo.
The lads could not believe it, as the crowd cheered. Mayo gave Mel a big hug, I can't believe it! How did you know?"
Mel was crying, so Mr Dobbs explained that Mia had appeared to them to let them know that you would be arriving at the same place we first arrived at."
Fig said, "Yes, and I knew that place was here because I will never forget that day for the rest of my life."
Rose was crying, as she could see Fig and Mel with tears running down their faces. Everyone was get-

ting emotional, even Jacks.

Mr Dobbs spoke out again, "You must all stay standing in the same place, as you don't have long here."

"What do you mean?" said Mayo.

"As much as we want you to stay longer, Mia told us that you can only stay just to say your goodbyes as you have to carry on your journey or you may never get another chance."

Even though it was a happy time, it was also sad to say goodbye to everyone.

"How is it going at the inn?" Woodsey asked Rose.

"Great! Jacks and his friends are running it now and we are the new landlords, thanks to all of you and Mr Dobbs of course."

Mr Dobbs nodded it was my pleasure."

They didn't have much time left, so Mel, Rose, Fig, Big Henry, Mr Dobbs and Helena all gave the lads a hug, while Jacks and his friends stood back and lifted their hands up as a thank you gesture. Fig put a brown parcel on the floor next to the lads.

"What's that?" asked Campbell.

"It's the clothes you came in. Don't want you going home like that, no one will recognise you."

"Thanks Fig," said Chrissy. "We're all going to miss you."

"We are all going to miss you too," said Mel.

As they all gave their last waves and kisses, little did they know that Mia was watching and even though she was in a trance a tear was rolling down her face. When Mia could see that they had all said goodbye, she started the process of getting them home. A gust of wind built up around the lads and a mist appeared again. Mel and Fig were sobbing as the lads faded away from sight. Soon they had totally disappeared. Mel and Fig hugged each- other and Rose put her arms around both of them and kissed the top of their heads to comfort them.

"I'm glad you met them, Fig," said Rose, "and brought them into our lives."

"Me too," said Mel, "it must have been meant to happen."

Big Henry turned to Jacks, "I don't know about you, but I could do with a drink."

"I'll second that," said Jacks.

"Come on, the first drink is on me," said Rose, to the crowds delight as they all cheered and made their way back to the Ship Inn.

CHAPTER NINE

The lads were still spinning which seemed to take even longer this time. They were still holding hands in a circle and strangely enough the brown parcel was floating in the middle of them. Things started to slow-down and they were soon standing on firm ground again. There was a mist around them, but it started to clear. As it cleared, they were back in Dovecot park, Liverpool, but there was nobody about, just like when they left, what seemed like a long time ago. As they caught their breath again, Woodsey said, "We might as well change back into our own clothes, while the place is empty."

"Good idea," said Gaffo.

"I think I'll leave mine on," said Chrissy.

"Trust you," said Campbell, "you will stick out like a sore thumb."

"I don't care, I will change when I get home, I will say I've been to a fancy-dress party."

"What as a chimney sweep." Said Woodsey.

This put a smile on everybody's face.

"Quick, let's get changed then," said Mayo, "has Fig put our trainers in?"

"Yes, he has," said Gaffo.

Just as they got changed back into their own clothes, the park looked as it should, full of people walking their dogs and kids playing. It was just as it was the day they left. In fact, it was the same day, with the same people and the same record playing on the radio.

"It's amazing," said Woodsey, "it's like we have never left."

"That means no one has missed us," said Campbell.

"At least we don't have to explain where we have been," said Woodsey.

As they walked away from the tree Chrissy looked back.

"Look over there." Everyone turned around and there was Mia's face slowly fading away, she was smiling, and everyone smiled back at her. Then she disappeared.

"Well, seeing a smile on Mia's face, it must mean everything is okay," said Woodsey.

"Maybe she was happy to see us getting back home safe," said Mayo. "It was nice that we got to see them all in London again though."

"Yes, it was," said Campbell.

They all walked across Dovecot park.

"I'm starving," said Chrissy.

"I think we all are," said Woodsey, "Anyone got any proper money?"

"I've got a fiver left," said Gaffo, "Come on I'll treat you all to chips and a buttered barm."

"That sounds fantastic," said Chrissy. "I never thought I would miss chips so much my belly is rumbling."

Woodsey brought up the subject about the gold coins. They decided to share them equally between them, *but they must not let any of their families see them, they must hide them away.*

"How many are left?" said Chrissy.

"65, So that's 11 each," said Campbell.

"Well worked out, Einstein," said Chrissy.

"Shut your face," said Campbell.

"What are you going to do, walk through me?" said Chrissy.

"Stop clowning around you two said Gaffo. "I thought we had more than that,"

"We did, but before we left for China I gave Rose more coins, she didn't want them, but I insisted as they were more use to her and her family, which, as we found out, she was able to buy the inn. I didn't think you would mind," said Woodsey.

All the lads looked at each other and agreed it was the right thing to do.

Just as they got to the edge of the park a group of lads were shouting over to them.

"What are you wearing, Knob head?"

It was a bunch of trouble- makers and the leader was from another school. He was known as Ghost because his hair was as white as snow. He had a bad reputation and had never lost a fight.

"Do you think we still have our powers?" Chrissy whispered into Campbell's ear.

"We will soon find out," Campbell replied.
Ghost came over and squared up to Gaffo and said,
"Do you think you can use your kung fu crap on me."
Gaffo had a big smile on his face. Then Ghost looked towards Campbell and Chrissy.
"What are you two whispering about, You pair of puffs."
Gaffo started laughing.
"What's so funny kung fu man?" As he came closer to Gaffo their foreheads were touching and things were getting tense.
"Leave this to me," said Campbell.
"Oh, are you the big man now with your weird mates and him," Pointing at Chrissy, "With his strange clothes."
Campbell's expression didn't change.
"As I said, I will handle this."
A voice came from behind the group.
"Listen, just leave it,"
It was Fitzy, who was a friend of the lads and went to the same school. Woodsey noticed he had cuts on his face. He surmised this was probably done by Ghost. Woodsey asked Fitzy to join them and just as he was walking over Ghost shouted.
"Stay there or I'll smack you again."
Campbell moved closer to Ghost and said,
"Do you want to start on me and lose your reputation in front of your dickhead mates?"
Ghost launched at Campbell throwing punches, his fists flying, but Campbell dodged them all. He

remembered not to show off too much. Then he caught Ghost with a right-hand punch to his face. Ghost stumbled back but came back at Campbell. Campbell let him throw a few punches, but he missed on each occasion. Campbell was getting bored, so he hit Ghost with two quick punches to the face, which knocked him to the ground. Ghost was rolling around in agony with blood pouring from his nose. Campbell and Chrissy stepped towards Ghost's mates, all ten of them, and they all stood back not wanting to fight. Chrissy said,

"Come on I'm starving, let's get some chips." As he walked past Ghost lying on the floor, he knelt down, and patted him on the head.

"That's your reputation gone mate and we've got all these witnesses here to prove it, isn't that right lads?"

They all nodded their heads in fear.

"Right, let's go to the chippy," said Mayo.

They all walked towards the chippy and beckoned Fitzy to join them, to his delight. *Ghost and his mates had ganged up on Fitzy when he was on the way to the shops for his mum and stole his money, £2. Gaffo said he would give him the money when he got change from the chippy.*

Chrissy wasn't happy with that and ran back to catch up with Ghost and his gang.

Meanwhile, the rest of the lads and Fitzy went to the chippy. Gaffo ordered six portions of chips with plenty of salt and vinegar and buttered barms. Fitzy was worried about Chrissy and asked if he would be all right. He was told not to worry as Chrissy could handle himself. The next minute Chrissy came walking in.

"Here you go, Fitzy, here is your two quid."

"Thanks Chrissy. I can get me mum's soap powder now. Were they forthcoming giving you the money back?".

"Not at first, they needed gentle persuasion."

"And what did you do exactly?" asked Campbell.

"Well I just ran around them fast, not too fast, but fast, while slapping them on top of their heads, until they gave in and handed over the money."

"I would have loved to have seen that" Laughed Gaffo.

The girl behind the counter shouted, "Six chips and six buttered barms."

"That's me," said Gaffo.

"£3 please." Gaffo handed the money over.

"Right, shall we go back to the park and eat these?" said Mayo.

"Sounds like a plan," said Campbell.

Fitzy popped to the shop next door and got his mum's soap powder before joining the lads who were heading to the park.

"Where did you get those clothes from Chrissy," asked Fitzy.

"We found them in a parcel in the park," replied Chrissy.

"You all seem different, you have all changed, I just can't think what it is that is different about you all," said Fitzy.

"Well nothing is any different, we don't feel any different." Gaffo winked at the lads.

They all sat down on the grass to eat their chips. Fitzy was quite anxious looking around to see if Ghost and his mates were about. He had no need to worry, they wouldn't bother him ever again.

"These chips are lovely," said Chrissy, "it's been ages since I've had chips."

"Ages?" said Fitzy, "It was only yesterday when I saw you eating chips."

They all looked at each other while stuffing their faces.

"I mean, it seems like ages since I had chips," Chrissy said.

Fitzy shook his head, "You lot are acting very strange. There is definitely something going on."

"Just eat your chips and stop thinking so much," said Chrissy.

They all laughed, including Fitzy.

Soon they had finished their chips. Chrissy was licking the paper. Fitzy watched and thought to himself, he is eating them chips like he hadn't tasted chips in a long time. Must be all that playing football, gave him an appetite'. Then Fitzy got up to go home, as his mum needed the soap powder to do her washing. He thanked the lads again for helping him. The lads watched him as he walked across the park.

"So, said Gaffo, we do still have our powers."

"I know, it's great isn't it? said Campbell, "but I don't know when Woodsey will be able to use his, you don't see may tigers walking around Liverpool."

"Ha ha!" said Woodsey, "you won't be laughing when I get a job as a zoologist."

"And what makes you think you'll become a zoologist?" asked Gaffo.

"Because I can communicate with any animal," said Woodsey.

"Prove it," said Chrissy.

Woodsey looked upwards at the sky for a couple of seconds.

"What's he doing?" whispered Mayo.

Just then a sparrow landed on his head and the lads were amazed.

"Watch it doesn't shit on your head," said Campbell.

Everyone burst out laughing.

"How did you know you could do that," asked Mayo.

"I just knew I could, it was an instinct," replied Woodsey.

The park was empty by now except for an old man walking his dog, but he was just leaving.

They thought it would be a good idea to try out their powers. Gaffo went first. He held out his hands towards the park bench concentrating intensely. Suddenly, the bench began to shake.

"You won't move that, it is bolted to the floor,"

said Chrissy.

You could see a little smirk on Gaffo's face as the bolts shot out of the floor and the bench floated over to them.

"Wow!" said Campbell, "that was brilliant!"

Gaffo was sweating and said, "Okay, let's see what you can do."

Campbell walked over to a tree and walked straight into it and vanished. The lads looked on in astonishment. They got closer to the tree. All they could see was his face on the trunk of the tree like a mirage.

"Okay, you can come out now, you're starting to scare me," said Chrissy.

Campbell stepped out of the tree and said, "I wonder if we can still run fast and jump high."

"Try it," said Woodsey.

Just then Campbell did a quick sprint and when he came back towards them, he jumped and landed on the top of the main branch.

"You look like Steve Austin," said Woodsey.

Next thing they were all jumping up into the tree having a good old laugh, getting carried away and enjoying themselves.

They heard a voice, "I knew there was something different about you lot." Fitzy appeared from behind the tree.

"Here's to keeping it a secret," said Woodsey.

"What secret?" asked Fitzy.

"You wouldn't believe it if we told you," said

Gaffo

"Try me," said Fitzy.

"Let's just say we have abilities, and you mustn't tell anyone about it. If you do tell anyone Chrissy will whistle at you.

Fitzy looked confused, *whistle at me, he thought, what will that do?*

So, Chrissy demonstrated what he could do by whistling. There was a rat by the bin and Chrissy whistled at it. The rat squealed and then went up in flames. I think Fitzy got the message. He swore he wouldn't tell anyone what he had witnessed.

They all made their way to the park gate. Woodsey felt a strange feeling come over him. He looked at Gaffo and knew he felt the same. In fact, they all felt it except for Fitzy. This could only mean one thing Mia was with them. But why would she be there, so soon after the lads had got back home?

"Can anyone sense Mia right now?" said Woodsey. They all nodded except for Fitzy.

"What's going on?" No sooner did Fitzy open his mouth his eyes went into a blank stare.

"What's happening to Fitzy?" said Chrissy, "it looks like his brain has left his head."

"That happened years ago," said Mayo.

"No, it's not funny," said Gaffo, "what's wrong with him?"

"He's okay," said Mia as she appeared to them.

"Why are you here?" asked Woodsey, "is everything okay at home?"

"Yes, everything is okay at home. I have been here since you arrived back to see how you would all cope and I must say, I'm not happy with you all. Within a short time of you being home you have been using your powers and I did warn you all that if it gets to be public knowledge, your lives will never be the same. I have erased Fitzy's memory and when he comes around, he will not remember what he has seen you all doing. You must be much more careful in the future because I won't be here to help you all next time. Promise
me you will all take better care in future."
They all made a promise to Mia that they would be careful not to show off their powers and they vowed they would keep to it. Mia bowed her head, "I must go now, but before I go, Chrissy would you put your normal clothes back on." And in a flash, she was gone.
Woodsey laughed, "Who would have thought Mia had a sense of humour? I think she is right though Chrissy you do stand out."
With that, Chrissy changed his clothes.

Fitzy was still in a trance, his eyes wide open in a glazed stare. Campbell clapped his hands in front of his face and Fitzy woke up instantly.

"What's going on?"

"What do you mean?" said Chrissy.

"I don't know. I remember going back to mine with me mum's soap powder and now I'm here."

"You've been daydreaming again Fitzy," said Mayo.

"I'm going home, I don't feel very good."
Then Fitzy made his way home, saying bye to everyone and that he would see them the next day.

"It was lucky that Mia did watch us for a bit, because we all know Fitzy can't keep a secret to save his life."

"You're right, said Woodsey, "everyone would have found out about us within ten minutes of him finding out."

The lads were all tired by now and wanted to go home to their comfy beds. They would all meet the next day in Dovecot park about 1 pm. Woodsey would be home from work by then, he liked working with his dad. Even though they had the gold coins, which were worth a lot of money. They wouldn't be able to sell them until they were much older, otherwise they would raise suspicion. They could be accused of having stolen them. They agreed they would keep the coins safe.

Woodsey and Gaffo walked down Pilch Lane towards the Greyhound pub, as they lived close to each other. Campbell and Chrissy walked off towards the Boundary pub, they also lived close to each other. Mayo jumped on the number 75 bus, he was a Huyton boy, but had moved to Fairfield with his family.

On the way home Gaffo said to Woodsey that things would never be the same. *It was going to be hard keeping their secret, but they had to, or their lives wouldn't be their own anymore. The world was their oyster, they could run faster than any athlete or footballer and jump higher than the top Olympic high jumpers. It will be frustrating knowing they would'nt be able to use their powers and strengths. They would discuss it the next day. They were looking forward to sleeping in their own beds. Everyone will think they had only been out for five hours when really, they had been away for weeks.It felt really strange.*

Woodsey turned into Newenham Crescent, while Gaffo carried on to the end of Pilch Lane. Woodsey put his key in the door and as the door opened, he could smell steak. He took a deep breath through his nose.

"I haven't smelt food that good in ages."

His mum was walking down the stairs, "What do you mean? You had a lovely pan of scouse last night."

"Oh yeah, I forgot."

His mum shook her head, "You worry me sometimes." As she walked past him into the kitchen to plate the food.

After Woodsey finished his food he said, "I'm going to bed now."

"Already? You must be tired," said his dad.

"I am. I must have played too much football today."

"I'll set the alarm for 4:30 am. See you in the morning," said his dad.

Back at the other lads' houses, they were settling

down for the night. All of them were very tired and wondering what was going to happen next. Campbell put his hand up while lying on his bed and put his fingers into the wall. Mayo was sitting on his bed looking straight through the wall to what was going on in the street. Gaffo was lying on his bed listening to his Walkman while a tennis ball was hovering above his hands. Chrissy was staring out of his bedroom window. He was about to start whistling but thought better of it. Woodsey was thinking of what situations the tiger was going to get in. He was thinking what lay ahead for the five young men who had these fantastic individual talents of speed and agility. Just before he went to sleep his last thoughts were what was going to become of his friends and what had happened to all the people they had met, especially, Mia, Chan, Fig, Mel,and Rose Maybe, just maybe, they would all meet again one day.

DESCRIPTION
Let your mind wonder as you follow the five young men from
Liverpool go on an adventure of a lifetime.

A story filled with history mixed with fantasy and a lot of fiction.
If you like a story with Warlocks, Wizardry, Time Travel, Superhero's
and a lot of action. Sit back, put your feet up and enjoy

Printed in Great Britain
by Amazon